Praise for *Redbirds, Roses, and Ghosts*

REDBIRDS, ROSES, AND GHOSTS celebrates the writer in all of us. With grace, humor, and compassion, Gayle Young captures a lost time for women and their "set-aside" dreams. Part memoir, part dream, the book travels to the past and what might have been, never losing sight of the power of a mother-daughter bond.
—Carolyn Haines, *USA Today* bestselling author

This is a charmer of a book, a memoir interspersed with short stories and poems, all inspired by Gayle Young's efforts in her first year of retirement to begin her life as a writer, come to terms with her past, and find humor in her daily life and family. She talks to ghosts, writes a novel, hears tempting desserts calling her name, and takes us along with her as she comes to realize that living in the past and worrying about the present are actually much less fun than appreciating and enjoying the life she has and the future she is beginning to imagine.
—Jennifer Horne, Alabama Poet Laureate

Gayle Young has created a fictionalized memoir that focuses on problems newly retired women face in trying to find a place for themselves. Insecurities, society's expectations, and changing lifestyles echo, one off the other, until the narrator is able to face who she is without regret. . . . At times, the reader, like the narrator, has difficulty deciding if the speaker is real or imagined. Young's ability to move from reality to fiction shows her to be a sure-footed storyteller. She has the power to grip our attention and let us know that the narrator's experiences are becoming more universal in the lives of today's women.
— Laura Hunter, author of *Beloved Mother*

REDBIRDS, &ROSES, GHOSTS

A MEMOIR

GAYLE YOUNG

This work is based on the author's personal perspective and
imagination.

Editor – Sierra Tabor
Interior & Illustration Design – Maria Yasaka Beck
Cover Illustration – Gennady Muradin
Managing Editor – Angela Broyles

Dedicated to the memory of Mother, Brother, and Chick, who, through all the ups and downs, laughter and tears, were always with me and loved me unconditionally.

CONTENTS

"We don't stop playing because we grow old; we grow old because we stop playing."

~ George Bernard Shaw

"The best remedy for those who are afraid, lonely or unhappy is to go outside, somewhere where they can be quiet, alone with the heavens, nature and God. Because only then does one feel that all is as it should be."

~ Anne Frank

REDBIRDS,
& ROSES,
GHOSTS

DISCLAIMER

This is a memoir based upon my reality, which may or may not have anything to do with actual reality. The characters in these stories are real and any similarity to other persons, living or dead, is purely intentional. Some of the names have been changed to protect the innocent and not so innocent. Most of the situations and incidents actually happened, some did not, and others are greatly exaggerated. Only my children and I know the difference, and they don't know everything.

one

TO DO OR NOT TO DO...
WHAT WAS THE QUESTION?

When I left work for good, I had two goals: finish the novel I'd started twenty years ago and lose twenty pounds. In one year. How difficult could it be?

After all, I'd been looking forward to retirement since my first day at my first part-time job at a small shoe store when I was sixteen. I must've done something wrong while putting money in the cash register, and to this day I can't figure out what it was. The manager, a tall, thin, brown-haired man with a constant scowl on his skinny face, turned red and muttered curse words under his breath while he jerked his ring of a thousand keys, stuck one in the cash register, fiddled, fumbled, and told me I should probably concentrate on my school work, that he had too many employees anyway, and it was okay if I didn't show up anymore.

Total humiliation. Abject failure. My first job had lasted about two hours. What would I tell my parents? What if I never found a job I could do and they had to support me the rest of my life? Would I still have an 11:30 p.m. curfew when I was thirty-five? I'd have to marry a rich man and spend my life lying on the sofa, eating chocolate turtles, and getting fat.

Unlike today, in the late 1950s most teenagers didn't have their own cars. As I trudged to the bus stop and waited in the hot sun for its arrival, with my burning skin, damp hair, and heart full of resentment, I plotted bodily harm to that bony manager. It was all his fault anyway. He should've told me new employees weren't allowed near the cash register, and besides, he was so skinny and prissy I figured I could take him in a fight. Of course then, as now, I hated violence and could barely stand to watch Roy Rogers or Gene Autry punch out the bad guys. No, who was I kidding? I'd never see that mean old man again, and if I did, I'd run in the other direction. But I could do to him what I did to everyone who "done me wrong." I'd write a story about him. He'd be screaming at a poor, innocent young woman and a whole shelf of shoes would fall on him and maim him for life. He deserved it for ruining my life and a possible career in shoe selling.

A few years later, I did get married, but he wasn't rich, and I did find a job that I could actually do. No cash exchanges. No cash registers. While at work in the law office, however, as I typed seemingly endless briefs, scheduled court dates, and answered telephones and mail, I dreamed of babies and a June Cleaver life. Every day I'd dress up, complete with high heels and pearls, and effortlessly cook gourmet meals, clean the house to a spotless shine, and, while my little bundle of joy napped, I'd have plenty of time to write short stories, maybe even a novel. Now that was fantasy. It's a wonder I didn't conjure up bluebirds sitting on my finger singing while cute little deer and rabbits talked to me.

As it turned out, I barely had the time or energy to dress, much less put on jewelry and shoes. Gourmet dinners and a clean house? They existed only in the section of my brain dedicated to "things to do." I left my job at the law office and didn't dream of going back to work while I was raising my children. I loved being with them. The other stuff? Not so much. I did sometimes envision my whole family being sucked up into an alien spaceship and transported to another planet, one where robots cleaned the house, bathed the children, cooked dinner, and took out the trash. While changing dirty diapers or cleaning a highchair smeared with stuff too gross to describe, I created alternate universes in my head where women ruled the world and men had PMS. When my children were arguing and fighting so loud my nosy neighbor called to see what was going on, I escaped into the old west, where a mob of unruly men with guns were about to hang an innocent, but oh so handsome, young man.

Over the years, the story whisperer in my head never gave up, like it knew that family always came first and someday its time would come. But as the children grew up and, one-by-one, left home and I re-entered the work force, it became louder, more persistent, and a lot more annoying. Then, one rainy spring day, while I was alone in my office and trying to organize my desk (emphasis on trying), Walter, the antagonist in my unfinished novel, laughed and said, "I'm going to get away with it."

"I don't think so," I answered audibly, looking around to be sure no one heard me.

"Who's going to stop me?"

"I am," I said.

"When?"

Well, Walter certainly was getting arrogant. I'd have to take him down a peg or two. "Tonight."

Of course, that night I couldn't find the unfinished manuscript. I remembered putting it in a safe place, so I wouldn't lose it. But where? Oh well, I could write a scene where Walter didn't get away with crime and mayhem and place it in the document later. I headed for the computer.

For a long time I stared at the screen. No pictures or words entered my head. *Okay, Walter, you pervert, where are you?* Maybe I was too tired. After all, I did my best work in the morning, but that was when I had to get ready for work. Maybe it was time to retire. But what if I retired and Walter or the story whisperer never came back? What would I do in those endless stretches of time I'd always dreamed about? For weeks, I muddled over the decision. My daughter, the one who likes to organize, suggested I make a list of pros and cons. So, I started making lists.

PROS AND CONS OF RETIRING:

Pros: (1) More time with grandchildren. (2) More time to write short stories and finish my novel. (3) More time to go to the library and study and learn new things. And (4) more time to clean the house.

Cons: (1) I might have to actually clean the house, including the overstuffed closets and vacuuming under the bed and behind the couch. (2) What if my creativity had deserted me and I couldn't really write and I'd have no excuses left for not writing?

I also made a list of all the things I'd learned during my lifetime, and I figured, if I left work, I could add to it.

MY LIST OF ALREADY-LEARNED,
HARD-EARNED LIFE LESSONS:

One - Never try to cut a frozen turkey.

Two - Children don't have to eat beets to grow up strong and healthy.

Three - Never give up on your dreams.

Four - Like Abe Lincoln, I think most of us are about as happy as we make up our minds to be, and, like Mark Twain, I've had many trials and tribulations in my life and some of them actually happened.

Five - Vengeance is futile. Thinking about tying your ex to a tree and setting it on fire or drowning your boss in a vat of boiling olive oil is very, very bad and doesn't hurt anyone except the thinker of the vengeful thoughts.

Six - Eat veggies and fruit and exercise every day. Throw in a few desserts every now and then, but not the entire chocolate cream pie after last night's pizza just because you have writer's block.

Seven - You really can catch more flies with honey than with vinegar.

Eight - We should listen to our children at least as much as we lecture them. Otherwise, like my own children, they'll number the lectures, call out that number, and zone out on you. When you scream "What did I tell you?" they'll tell you. Verbatim.

Nine - This one I owe to Wayne Dyer: Given a choice between being right and being kind, always choose kindness.

Ten - No one ever learned anything by being yelled at.

Eleven - Think positive.

Twelve - Laughter is the best medicine, after all.

Thirteen - Be grateful. Every day.

THINGS I WOULD LIKE TO DO WHEN I RETIRE:

One - Spend more time with my grandchildren.

Two - On this exact date next year, have my novel finished and be twenty pounds thinner.

Three - Take literature classes and figure out what Steinbeck and Fitzgerald have that I don't.

Four - Take computer classes and, hopefully, learn the art of copying and pasting Word documents into an email while maintaining the formatting.

Five - Read books on how to organize—no, probably not. That's taking things too far.

As my working days drew to a close and the final hours were in sight, I spent more and more time dreaming about my glorious carefree days. While everyone else was getting ready for and driving to work, I'd sit on the back porch, sip coffee, listen to the sounds of nature, meditate, and compose poetic prose. I'd cook a healthy breakfast, take the dog for a walk, lift weights, and then, during that glorious stretch of precious time to myself, I'd sit at the computer while perfect words flowed from my brain through my fingers and into the Word document.

two

COFFEE, ROSES, AND (FINALLY) TIME

Of course, that's not exactly how that first day went. I did wake up early, however. I brewed my favorite French vanilla coffee, doused it with sugar and cream, and ambled to the screened-in back porch. Ahhh. Life was beautiful. Cicadas and redbirds serenaded me, and my roses sported red, yellow, and peach-colored blossoms. A blue jay squawked and chased our orange cat across the yard while my loveable dog of unknown breed, Dixie, slept in the chaise lounge.

Yep, I was going to love the retired life. Time to get serious about my writing. Except, I hadn't counted on my first day of freedom being the hottest day on record. It was mid-July down south, and at 6:30 in the morning, it was already 88 degrees and 70 percent humidity, with the heat index forecast around 110. I flipped on the ceiling fan, inhaled the aroma of my coffee, sipped its sweet richness, and closed my eyes to think profound and spiritual thoughts. Beads of perspiration popped out on my forehead and slid down my face. I wiped at them with the back of my hand and tried to concentrate on my breathing.

Just then Dixie jumped from her chaise lounge and wiggled out through the doggy door barking. The dog next door joined her, and soon there was a neighborhood canine choir howling at the siren in the distance that Dixie had heard long before I did. My eyes popped open and refused to close again until she shut up and lay down in the middle of what was left of my ailing, thirsty, iris plants.

On the other side of the yard, a sparrow pecked at a dried leaf that was flatter but bigger than he was. The leaf must've caught on his beak because the little fellow tossed it from one side to the other until, finally, it broke free and he hopped to another dead leaf. A redbird perched on the fence post and appeared to be watching the whole thing.

Okay, back to meditating. I closed my eyes. Thank You, God, for… for. Geez, it was hot for so early in the morning. Thanks for… I wondered if I paid the electric bill. Streams of sweat dribbled down my neck and chest and into my bra. My t-shirt clung to me; my breasts itched. As I lifted my shirt and scratched between my breasts, Dixie stared at me. I looked around to see if my next-door neighbor Jack, who scrutinized the comings and goings of every female within his field of vision, had also watched.

He hadn't, but my husband, Clay, had. "So, what're you going to do all day?" he asked.

My lips pouted, and my eyes squinted. I glared at him, my meanest look, and I wanted to tell him I was about to start writing a best-selling novel when he had interrupted my train of thought, but I didn't get the chance.

Instead of waiting for an answer, he kissed, no pecked, me on the lips and disappeared into the garage then out into the frenetic traffic, on his way to join all the other people who still worked for a living instead of sitting around wiping at sweat, doing nothing.

But doing nothing was okay. It gave my imagination an opportunity to come to life. A fly circled my head. I swatted at it. It flew around and settled on the table. "How'd you get in?" I screamed and swatted at it again. Elusive little devil. It darted from the table to my hair and, while I was slapping at my head, it hovered over my coffee cup.

I couldn't take this meditating any longer. Maybe I should clean the kitchen while I got my thoughts together. On the way to the sink, I passed the refrigerator.

It didn't say a word, but it called to me. Tempted me with visions of half a chocolate pie hidden behind a container of broccoli with cheese sauce. No, Gayle, you can't. Not for breakfast. Go to the sink, straight to the sink. Do not look back. I opened the door and stood there like a zombie, staring and waiting for something healthy and delicious to jump out at me. Wilted salad in a bag? Ugh. Watery, diet strawberry gelatin? Yuck. The broccoli? Definitely not.

But what about the Bud Light behind it? To me, beer had always tasted worse than a glass of Listerine, yet ever since I heard that alcohol enhances creativity, I'd wanted to try it. But this early? Even my Aunt Sadie didn't drink at 7:00 in the morning. Still, one has to make sacrifices for the sake of one's art. Besides, who would know? Slowly, I pulled the cold can from its hiding place, popped its top, and, with my stomach already feeling queasy, hesitantly drew it to my mouth and gulped. Then spewed. All the way to the sink. Ugh. Yuck. Beer all over my shirt, the floor, and the counter. I swished water in my mouth as I sprinted around the kitchen. It didn't help. My stomach gurgled and churned and, finally, settled down.

With half a chocolate pie in hand, I settled back into my chair on the back porch, this time ready to write. I gazed absentmindedly at the faint blue lines on the first page and traced my fingers across the spiral binding of the college-lined notebook with a picture of three golden retriever puppies on the front that I'd bought especially for this day. To start the writing process, I drew a heart at the top of the page, followed by a five-pointed star and arrows pointing in both directions.

Finally, I wrote, "It's hot this morning. Sunny and humid." Well, that was certainly poetic. Two redbirds, male and female, chased each other across the yard and disappeared into the trees. *Think, Gayle, write*. Nothing. "Next winter I'll probably complain about the cold." I stared at Dixie as she turned and twisted on her chaise lounge, curled into a ball, and settled back in exactly the same spot.

For years, the characters in my mind had clamored for attention, plotting murder and mayhem and imploring me to let them out. They told me who they were, where they lived, and what they wanted to do—some of it not legal or virtuous. Where were they now? And why in the world was I doing this? Where was Heather—the ethereal 19th century heroine who resided in my mind and begged me to write her story—when I really needed her? And where in the world was that devil, Walter?

What force had kept me writing gibberish or short stories in my notebook that I was afraid would never be good enough to be published? Maybe I read too much. Or maybe it was the fault of Mrs. Ford, my English teacher in seventh grade. One day she told us to write a play, and she promised she'd pick the best one to be performed for our class. She picked mine.

It was about two kids who defied their parents and explored the neighborhood "haunted" house. They got stuck in the basement, and the rest of the play was about their attempts to get out in time to get home for supper so their parents wouldn't know what they'd been up to.

Little did I know that play would affect me immediately and for the rest of my life. I started writing short stories before school, during recess, in study hall, and at night while I pretended to be doing my homework. Especially then. I wrote about the events of the day: "Got into trouble at school for passing notes." Or "It rained so hard, Mrs. Gimmell's (gym teacher) shoes got wet, and she squeaked when she walked." To get ideas, I eavesdropped on strangers, family, and friends, read true crime and romance magazines I sneaked from Mother's room, and spied on my brother who was five years older than me and was my protector.

When the boy across the street picked on me, Brother picked on him. When Brother sneaked into the cornfield with his girlfriend, I followed. Occasionally, a good story about him and his current girlfriend was worth blackmail money. The Brother story I remember best, though, was when he was in junior high and I was in second or third grade. We went to the same school, only in different sections of the building.

The infamous race occurred on a cool, damp, overcast day just before Halloween, or at least my memory has delivered it to me that way for years. He, our cousin Jimmy, and a couple of friends raced home from school every day to see who could run the fastest. Brother always lost. He desperately wanted to win.

Between home and the school was an abandoned cemetery with overgrown bushes, giant weeds, and weather-beaten headstones covered with vines and moss. Many of the headstones were overturned or leaning. Most of the graves were sunken and formed long narrow bowls filled with decaying leaves and debris. The overhanging canopy of trees made the whole area perpetually dark and spooky. There was, of course, always an accompanying moldy odor and clammy humidity that clung to young skin. I only took that shortcut on days when some kid dared me to, and then I ran as fast as I could.

Brother always ignored me if I happened to wander over to his side of the school building. He didn't just pretend I wasn't his sister; he acted like I didn't exist. The day of the infamous race, I spotted him and a few friends in an animated discussion, and when I got to the outer realm of their kingdom, I heard Jimmy say, "So, you too chicken?" Then he clucked and flapped his arms.

Brother looked around, pushing at the hair that fell over his forehead. He changed his books from one hand to the other, clearly stalling for time, trying not to appear scared. In the midst of dares and jeers and shouts of "yellow" and "chicken," he took a few steps in the direction of the cemetery and said, "Sure, I'll go. Too bad you're too chicken to go with me."

"I ain't chicken," said Jimmy. "You're just scared to go by yourself."

"Chicken."

Cheers, taunts, and laughs from the crowd. Jimmy had no choice.

He and Brother slowly entered the path that led through the woods to the cemetery. The rest of us ran around to the other side of the wooded area. Just as we got there, Brother busted out of those woods, passed us, and for the first and only time, he beat everyone home. Jimmy was a close second. It seems a ghost had jumped out from behind one of the tombstones, screeching and wailing and rattling chains.

In all the excitement and chaos of running after Brother and Jimmy, I could've been mistaken, but I still have this fleeting memory of Mrs. Turner, Brother's history teacher, walking out of the woods, laughing. She was a short, skinny, white-haired waif of a woman who smelled like gardenias and looked like she could barely lift a pencil, but she always left boys twice her size quivering in their seats.

Several years later, when I had her for history, Mrs. Turner told me she remembered Brother fondly, but for some reason she delighted in humiliating me. "Gayle, go out in the hall to finish your performance," she said when she caught me chewing gum. "Alright, Miss Gayle, you know all the answers. Now tell the class what finally got the U.S. into World War II." I had been whispering.

"Gayle, let me see that." She jerked the note I was trying to pass to my friend, Becky. "Well, new boy, she thinks you're the cutest."

The new boy turned red while twenty-seven pairs of eyes focused on me, and the giggles in the room sounded like a swarm of yellow jackets.

In class the next day, Mrs. Turner told us to read a chapter in *The Diary of Anne Frank*. I actually liked that book and was going to read it, but I was still mad at Mrs. Turner, so some devil made me compare her to a Nazi soldier. With my book standing up in front of me, I took out my notebook and described her as a mean, ugly person, but in my story, I was the heroine who captured and tied her up and threw her into a river. She got away, but I rode on horseback and jumped on her back as she ran, wet and dirty, toward the railroad tracks and an oncoming train.

"What are you writing?" I looked up. Mrs. Turner stood over my desk, staring at the paper.

"Nothing." I quickly covered the errant words with my forearms.

"I thought I told you to read Chapter 3." She tapped the desk with a ruler. "You'll be the first person I call on during discussion."

Those same twenty-seven pairs of eyes again focused on me. This time there were no giggles, just stares of pure terror. True to my m.o., I burst into tears, jerked my notebook, and ran from the room.

The next day, class hadn't even started yet when Mrs. Turner stood over me, tapping her ruler against my desk. "Gayle, what in the world are you writing now?"

Quickly, I closed my notebook and answered. "It's about Anne Frank."

"Would you care to read it to the class?"

"No, ma'am."

"Are you going to run out crying if I tell you to?"

"Yes, ma'am."

She gave me her wickedest smile and moved on to the new, cutest boy behind me.

Funny, but all those years later, I could still see Mrs. Turner's face, her wrinkles with face powder in the creases, her gray eyes and mischievous smile. As I sat there on my back porch, it dawned on me. She knew all along what she was doing and enjoyed doing it. She taught me history. I remember a lot about World War II, not necessarily the facts and dates, but its horrors and human toll, its heroes and sacrifices, and, because of her, what it must've been like for my uncles at Normandy.

And Mrs. Ford? Did she know what she was doing when she chose my play? Did she mean to plant that seed in my mind? I'd spent a lifetime writing, jotting down words and sentences whenever I found the time, pouring my confusion, anger, pain, accomplishments, and joy onto the pages of notebooks and scraps of paper. I still had those notebooks, and now I had time to read them and turn them into the short stories that had been rolling around in my head for years and finish that novel I'd started twenty years ago.

three

TEMPTATION

The next morning, armed with coffee, notebook, and pen, and with renewed fervor, I sat at the round patio table on the back porch and gazed at the redbirds, sparrows, and robins, at the roses, and at a wasp trying desperately to get through the screen to its outside world. Time to resume my inner storyline and this time actually write something. Stacks of laundry filled my head. I tapped my pen against the black metal of the table. Nothing. I doodled on the college-lined paper. My stomach growled. I stared at the blue jay, again swooping down and shrieking at our orange cat that was scurrying to get to the doggie door.

My fervor faded. Just like that. After years of planning, panic set in. I now had all day every day, my dream come true, but where was the creativity that had lived inside me while I worked and raised children? Poems had skipped across my mind as I drove through traffic; short stories had presented themselves to me complete with beginning, middle, and end as I changed diapers. Eloquent words had flowed while I scrambled eggs or rinsed endless stacks of dishes and loaded them into the dishwasher.

Maybe I'd waited too long to write them down. I was too old. My mind wasn't as sharp or creative as it used to be, and I couldn't drink beer. Now what? Tired and distressed, I closed my eyes and tried to meditate on the word "love," to me synonymous with God, and listen. Yes, there was a voice, a quiet whisper, but it was saying… fried chicken?

Now, the thing about retirement is its close proximity to that darned refrigerator. Again, like the previous morning, it called to me. I tried not to listen. Write, Gayle, write. I thought about the fried chicken still in its cardboard basket. Shame to let it go to waste, and it might make me feel better. No. Couldn't even think it. I doodled an elaborate curved arrow. Potato salad left over too. Back to writing. Zero inspiration.

Ahhhh. Nothing like the aroma of a crispy chicken leg warming in the toaster oven. It could've been a nostalgic moment, bringing back stories of my grandmother and her famous fried chicken, if Dixie would quit barking and trying to get to the toaster oven. Before we found her, someone must've hit her with a kitchen appliance. She barked at all humming, clicking, swooshing machines and even at the iron and ironing board, which made no sound at all.

We'd found her, skinny and dusty, in the Winn-Dixie parking lot. We didn't know what she was, and the vet didn't either. She looked sort of like a miniature German shepherd with a corgi tail and a bit of pinscher coloring. The vet's office put "Heinz 57" on their records.

Whatever she was, she loved me, her rescuer. When I went to the back porch, she followed; when I went to the bathroom, she followed, and when we went for a walk, she barked at everyone who came near me. Although she'd never attacked or bitten anyone, her bark was a bit menacing. When they saw us coming, my neighbors waved and moved to the other side of the road. When salesmen came to my door, I let her stand beside me and bark. They always smiled and backed down the sidewalk.

That morning, Dixie wagged her tail and followed me and the chicken leg to the family room where I settled into the soft, beige cushions on the couch. I pinched off a bite of chicken for myself and gave one to Dixie. Another for me; one for her. In an effort to rid myself of the enveloping melancholia, I turned on the TV and flipped through channels.

That's when I discovered reruns of *The Waltons* and *Little House on the Prairie,* my all-time favorite shows. For four hours, two episodes of each, I languished there, caught up in the dramas of John Boy and Laura, while longing for my own little ones or at least my recently vacated job. To ease the pain, I consumed a small bag of potato chips and a twelve-ounce Diet Coke in addition to the chicken.

All of that, however, didn't diminish my appetite. At noon, while sitting at the kitchen counter and watching the mid-day news, I ate a ham sandwich and finished off the potato salad. I figured I'd wait until the next morning when my mind was fresh to start writing again, but maybe I could do something productive, like organizing the hall closet. Right after I finished off the brownies that'd been around a couple of days.

After munching the brownies I was so tired I lay on the couch, with Dixie beside me, for a few minutes to rest and let my food digest before tackling the closet. Just in time, too. *Days of Our Lives* was coming on. When it was over, I extricated myself from the couch and headed toward the closet.

On the way, however, I passed the guest room/office and figured I might as well check my emails and bank balance. Instead, I clicked the Word icon, started going through my list of documents and opened a short story I had started right after my divorce. Maybe I could finish it. I read and reread that story, waiting for a word, sentence, or at least some insight as to which way the plot should go. Nothing came to mind. With pen and notebook in hand, I retreated to the back porch and stared at my empty bird feeder. Still nothing. Dixie nudged my leg, a stuffed dog toy that resembled a chipmunk in her mouth. For a few minutes I tapped my pen against the table. Nothing. I described the heat of the sun: "hot." The breeze of the ceiling fan: "cool."

Finally, I played tug-of-war with Dixie and went inside, intending to clean that nuisance closet, but as I passed the TV and couch, they called to me. Oh, well, maybe a break would help me generate new ideas. Wow, late afternoons were really interesting. That Dr. Phil guy tells it like it is, and Oprah, well, her show made me cry, so I had to have something to make me feel better. During the first commercial I searched the cabinets. No cookies, no chips, no leftovers. Desperation. At last I found a Dr. Pepper and some cheddar cheese which I melted on bread. Perfect.

When Clay came home that night, he found me still in the baggy, gray knit shorts and t-shirt I'd slept in, lying on the couch and watching the evening news. I was so fatigued I couldn't get up to cook dinner.

"What'd you do all day?" he asked, looking at the dishes still in the sink. He stared at the brownie crumbs, chicken bone, and remnants of the ham sandwich on the counter.

Bless Clay. I met him after my children were grown. I'd tried and failed Relationships 101 a number of times and had given up on men altogether. On a rainy day as I was headed to the dentist, in the overpass between the building where we both worked and the parking garage, Clay appeared. We stopped and talked about the leak in the roof of the overpass, and later that day he sent me an invitation to lunch on the back of his business card. I told my friend, "I hope he pays for lunch. I don't have enough money." He did.

He was quiet, never raised his voice or criticized me, and didn't try to change me. He seemed to like me the way I was. He let me be me. He still does.

After I gave him my meanest stare, he didn't scream or fuss or tell me I was lazy. He didn't ask, "Should I not ask you that question ever again in this lifetime?" or, "What's the matter with you?" He simply said, "Don't you feel well?" and went out and got us a couple of hamburgers and fries. No wonder I love him.

Of course, his response would've been different during football season, especially if Alabama was playing. Between late August and the Super Bowl, I was pretty much on my own. Good thing nothing bad had ever happened to me during an Alabama game. But what if it did? Would Clay wait until half-time to come to my rescue? Or would he leave immediately? Probably immediately. But he would be peeved… Hmm… I remembered writing a story about that very thing not too long ago.

THE PICNIC

The day I died, I went on a picnic. Alone. I'd asked Dan to go with me, but his reply was, "Nope, going to the Tavern. Alabama's playing."

It was our anniversary, and he'd forgotten again. I should've known it'd be like this when we had to plan our wedding around the football schedule. Mom had tried to warn me.

He gazed approvingly at his reflection in the bathroom mirror, smoothing his crimson shirt. Guess he didn't notice the gray in his brown hair or the wrinkles on his forehead. He smelled good, though, thanks to the sexy cologne I had given him. If he flashed enough cash, he might get some giddy young thing to pay attention to him.

He sucked in his stomach, took a last look at his image, and sauntered out the door. I lay on the bed and cried my last tears on Earth. My mind retrieved the picture of Dan the day he proposed to me. With a watermelon cooling in the flowing water of Turkey Creek, we had walked hand-in-hand through trees and bushes while he talked about our future home, babies, and how much he loved me. Not once had he mentioned football.

Dammit, if Dan wouldn't go, I'd go on a picnic by myself, and I wouldn't come home until way after the game was over. I'd make him wonder where I was. That'd teach him.

It was a bright cool day in late October. I sat on a large rock, breathed in the aroma of damp decaying foliage, and, with my bare feet dangling in the cold water, watched, mesmerized, as red, yellow, and brown leaves drifted downstream. That's when I saw her, a translucent apparition that looked like, "Mom?"

I stood up and stepped onto a dry spot on top of the next rock, aware only of the water whooshing around me and my mom on the other side of the creek, shouting, "Be careful! Those rocks are slippery!"

The last thing I remembered was hopping toward the next rock just before a sudden jolt of intense pain. Blackness. My eyes opened. I was looking up into a shimmering, golden light. Dazed and bewildered, I sat up and looked around, trying to get my bearings. My body didn't move. It lay face-down on the rocks. Blood oozed out of my head. My auburn hair and black jacket floated around me.

This couldn't be good. Panic. Fear. I didn't know what to do. But the light warmed and soothed me as Mom put her arms around me and said in a voice light and airy, "It's okay, baby, I'm here."

I looked at her. At my body. Back at her. "You died, Mom. Two years ago. Does that mean I'm…?" I couldn't say the word.

She nodded.

The flowing water threatened to dislodge my body. Until that minute I didn't know ghosts could get nervous and anxious. "Someone has to tell Dan. He's got to find me. I'm going to go bobbing away down this stream and it'll mess up my face. I'll look like hell at my funeral."

"Someone will tell him," she assured me.

That wasn't good enough. I saw a couple of teenage boys sitting on the bank smoking pot. I tried to march toward them but found myself sort of floating. "Hey, you guys!" I called out. "You gotta call somebody. You hear?"

I waved my arms in front of them. Did cartwheels. Ran back and forth through them and managed to get a few small pebbles to rain down on them.

"Did you feel that?" the skinny one in the black t-shirt with a skull on it said.

"Yeah, man, kind of creepy-like."

"I'm outta here."

Both jumped up, dropped their funny cigarettes, and ran.

"I want you to go with me toward the light," Mom said.

"Not yet. I've got to tell Dan." I intended to drive to the Tavern to find him, but when I started toward the car, I popped into the bar.

And discovered that ghosts have tempers. He was sitting at a table with a bleached blonde about half his age who was wearing a shirt that stretched the word Alabama to interesting proportions and shapes. Her foot touched his, and she whispered something in his ear. He laughed. With the rest of the crowd he jumped up, cheered, and yelled "Roll Tide!" Then he motioned for the waitress and ordered two more beers.

My worst nightmare. I was lying dead in a stream, and Dan was flirting with a bimbo.

"Remember, dear, you're dead. Don't do anything foolish," Mom said.

"I'll show him." I meant to get his attention. I tried to wallop him in the face. My hand went through him. I stomped on his head. Nothing. He didn't move his eyes from the screen until a time-out led to a commercial.

Miss Bimbo smiled seductively and leaned toward Dan. He leaned toward her and said, "Wilson's fumbled twice; think we'll see any of McElroy today?"

If looks could kill, he'd have joined me in the hereafter, but she smiled and said, "I don't know."

"Probably not," he said. "I don't know why Saban won't play McElroy. Give him a chance to prove himself."

She feigned interest. "I know what you mean."

Then romantic Dan delivered his famous pickup line, "Go, Arenas. Aw, great block! Did you see that? Arenas is amazing. And he's only a junior."

She moved away and sucked her blue drink.

I got in his face and said, "You've got to find me."

His answer: "Now, if Wilson can only hold onto the ball for a few plays."

"Really, baby, we have to go," Mom said.

"Not yet."

I ran through the bar, with Mom chasing me, through people, tables, and that electronic monster that ruined my marriage, smacking at glasses, liquor bottles, chips, and pretzels. The bartender swatted at the air around him when I buzzed through him. I made the lights go out. He clicked them back on. I turned them off. He began to get agitated, and the bar patrons started to pay attention. So I did it again and again. They stood up in unison and yelled very unkind words when the place went dark and cheered when it lit up. Expletives. Cheers.

I whisked through Miss Blonde Slut. She spilled her glass of blue stuff; it oozed down her tight shirt. I waved my hand through a black plastic bowl and sent peanuts flying across the room. That was so much fun I went to the bar and danced across it, sending chips and napkins sailing across the room while whiskey and beer poured down the bar.

The dazed bartender froze for a few minutes, quickly regained his momentum, and was the first one out the back door. The barflies quickly followed.

Finally, the room was cleared except for a few guys still staring at the screen, including Dan, who didn't notice Blondie had left and was saying, "Aw, Wilson, who were you throwing to?"

"Are you through with your tantrum?" Mom said, and I swear she sounded just like she did when I was a teenager.

"I just want him to care!" I cried.

"He does," she answered, sitting at the table with Dan. "He doesn't know."

I sat beside him. Not until the commercial came on did he look around. "What the hell? Where'd everybody go?" But still he didn't leave until the game was over.

"You're not going to go with me until he finds you, are you?"

"No."

"Very well." Mom and I instantly appeared at the creek again.

Immediately, a sheriff's deputy stopped his car and wandered around the area until he saw me and called an ambulance.

Mom and I went with him to tell Dan. I guess Alabama had won. He was sitting happily in front of the TV at home, watching the post-game wrap-up.

When the sheriff's deputy told him about me, he broke down. It was the first time I'd seen him cry since Alabama lost the SEC championship game.

Later that night, I lay beside him on the bed and listened as he called my name over and over, mumbling,

"Susan, I'm so sorry, baby. I should've gone with you. I love you."

"I told you so," Mom said.

"Did you have to say that?" I put my hands on my hips and stared into her eyes, just like I had when I was a teenager and gave her "the look."

"Do you want your face to freeze like that for eternity? Come on, we've got to go."

I hugged and kissed my husband one last time. He stroked his face as if he felt it and wiped at the tears in his eyes.

I turned toward Mom and said, "I'm grown now, and I don't have to do what you say," as we walked toward the light.

four

MEMORIES AND LABOR

When my eyes fluttered open on the third morning of my non-working workday, it was still dark. I turned over and tried to go back to sleep. No such luck. All those years of jumping out of bed, rushing to get ready, driving in the most irritating, aggravating traffic, and longing for the day when I could sleep late. No. It couldn't be. No, no, no, no.

Unfortunately, it's a fact of life. By the time you actually can sleep late, your bladder goes into overdrive. Persistent. Demanding. Do it now. Whimpering like a baby, I crawled out of bed and stumbled as fast as I could to the bathroom.

Later, while washing my hands, I studied my reflection in the mirror, the one with the perfect lighting that let me see myself as if I were thirty years old. No wrinkles. No sagging. No age spots. Of course, when I looked at pictures of myself away from the mirror, I always asked, "Who is that old lady?"

That morning, however, as I was admiring my image and blessing the lights and mirror, I made a momentous decision. As soon as I'd finished all those jars and tubes of expensive anti-aging creams and potions, I'd never buy another one. At my age, wrinkles happen. So what? And I'd let my hair go gray. I examined my salt and pepper roots and tried to picture how I'd look with that color, or rather, non-color, all over my head. No, I shouldn't get too carried away. I'd stick with the champagne blonde for a few more years. And maybe just one anti-aging cream.

I also decided that I wouldn't get caught up in the sitting, eating, and watching TV all day cycle. As soon as I had my coffee in hand, I'd get started on the hall closet, maybe find some of my old stories and that novel I'd quit work to finish.

That closet was mine, and no one in my family dared to open its door. For years I'd stuffed it full of boxes of pictures, crayon drawings my children and grandchildren had given me, baby clothes and shoes, cherished mementoes, and old clothes in various sizes. Somehow, someday just one of those shirts, blouses, suits, dresses, or pants would come back into style and I'd be exactly that size.

When sufficient caffeine coursed through the pathways of my brain, I dragged two boxes to the end of the hallway. Another one. After an hour or so, my hallway was lined with boxes marked "travel brochures and info," "Christmas," "old pictures," some with no descriptive information, and a couple with question marks. In the corner, I found a dirty tattered box with "Brother and Mother" printed in smudged black marker on the side and top. A wave of nostalgia washed over me. I had to open it.

The first thing I found inside was a dirty, white ceramic horse that Brother had won at the Alabama State Fair, its once bright blue, red, and gold saddle faded. Next, a tiny doll, about as tall as my hand. Wearing a bra and grass skirt, she stood on a seashell. When I was young, I could touch her hips and they would swing from side to side. I traced the saddle of the horse and then the doll's long black hair with my finger as if their touch would bring back my childhood.

Holding both of them to my chest, I slid down the wall and sat beside Dixie, who was curled into a ball. I ran my hand over her short, soft fur and cried, longing to see my brother and mother's faces, hear their voices, and hug them again. Dixie uncurled and licked me in the face and, though her breath smelled like rotten fish, her gesture made me smile. For a few minutes, I was a pre-teen again.

I sat again at my small maple desk that was cluttered with the treasures of my life—a green, locking diary I never wrote in; a pair of shiny purple house shoes, the only gift Daddy ever gave me; a jewelry box Mother had given me that played music while a ballerina in a pale blue tutu twirled around; and the gold stemmed lamp with the red velvet shade Mother had fashioned from an old bedspread. I held the notebook decorated with pictures of Elvis I'd cut from magazines. In it I'd written quickly whatever came to mind, feelings I wasn't allowed to express in polite company. Questions that had no answers. Thoughts I had been ashamed to think.

Questions from that pre-teen time flowed through my heart. Why did Mother and Daddy divorce? Why didn't Daddy love me? Is there really a God? If so, why in Old Testament times did He love only the Jewish people? Why didn't He love Egyptians or Chinese or Babylonians? And if He didn't love them, why did He create them? Was there really a hell?

When we studied fossil fuels at school and I learned it took millions of years for oil to form, I worried that we humans would deplete our resources, and then where would we be? I wrote a story about it with an ending where the grown-ups figured out a way for us to colonize Mars, so we could dig up all their oil and send it to Earth.

I had written in the notebook about the time Mother and I rode the bus across town to the Alabama State Fair.

At that time, 1950 I think, children were taught that if you were sitting and an adult walked into the room and there were no other seats, you were to get up and give that adult your seat. No exceptions.

That day the bus was crowded and smelled like exhaust fumes mixed with sweat and stale, cheap perfume. Mother and I sat up front on the long seat that faced the aisle. Across from us, a tall, blond-haired young man wearing a dark green uniform nodded as if he could barely stay awake. In the back, several people held onto the poles, bouncing, talking, complaining, and laughing as the bus chugged along.

At one stop, a stooped and wrinkled, gray-haired, African-American woman hobbled up the stairs. With her hands shaking, she dropped coins into the coin box and slowly crept toward the back of the bus. Immediately, I jumped up so she could sit. Before I was all the way up, however, Mother jerked me down.

"Why?" I asked her.

She clamped her hand on my thigh and stared straight ahead. The blond guy stared back, as if daring Mother to move or say anything. The bus driver's angry eyes filled the rearview mirror. A hush of quiet alarm filled the bus. I knew I'd done something wrong.

The old woman said nothing and looked at no one as she slowly made her way through the crowd of stiff white people to the back where she held onto one of the poles and tried to steady herself as the driver shifted gears abruptly and the bus jerked and continued its journey.

I wondered now if the old woman had been Lula, would Mother have reacted the same? Probably so. I think she had been genuinely afraid of the other people on the bus.

Like everyone else in our family, she loved Lula, the tall, dark-skinned, heavyset woman who helped Mother with canning, washing, ironing, housework, and me. Some of my earliest and happiest memories are of Lula applying mercurochrome to a skinned knee, hugging me and telling me I'd be fine. Almost every time she brushed my hair, she said "Now, Spruchie, if you don't sit still, I'm gonna snatch you bald-headed." Spruchie sat still. Brother loved her because when he tried to get out of the house without me and I cried and carried on, she distracted me with shiny metal pots and pans and wooden spoons.

Even after Mother and Daddy divorced and Lula no longer worked for us, she kept in touch and visited. Many times she sat at our table and had coffee or iced tea and cake or cookies. I've often wondered what happened to Lula. During the civil rights struggles of the 1960s, did her children or grandchildren take part? Did they tell her we were evil, not to be trusted? One time I wrote a story about her and my family and what it might have been like during that time, but somewhere in all my moving, I lost it. Like I lost her.

I laid the horse and doll aside and picked up a handful of old dingy papers, some in barely legible handwriting and some crudely typed stories I'd written when I was twelve or thirteen. Back then I'd thought they were pretty good. Now I realized they were childish, disjointed, and jumped from one thing to another without any sense of connection.

One heroine started on a journey to find a friend who'd disappeared. She had all kinds of adventures but somewhere along the way forgot her lost friend, where she was, and wound up on a space ship. Another heroine was lost in the woods alone and found a baby in a pink blanket.

The only prevailing, recurring theme seemed to be a search for something I'd once had and lost but couldn't remember what it was. My heroines didn't belong, were always going somewhere, and looking for something but never finding it. They forgot the plot and drifted off into something else. They were with someone they loved who disappeared. I'd tried to make it light, unnoticed, humorous, but underneath it was always there, like a sad dream that comes night after night in different forms.

Also in the box was a Chanel No. 5 bottle that had once contained Mother's favorite fragrance and one of her jewelry boxes filled with the clunky jewelry she loved: gold and silver earrings, necklaces, bracelets, and pins with bright, colorful stones, some of them real, some very good fakes.

I closed my eyes and tried to visualize her and Brother's faces. What I saw was myself, the skinny kid I used to be, freckle-faced with long, stringy, sandy-blonde hair, skipping down the sidewalk and wading through the gutter in the rain. I sat on the front steps of my first home, the only one my mother, father, brother, and I ever lived in together. Mother, so young and beautiful, with long, shiny dark hair and a perfect porcelain complexion, sat beside me and ruffled my hair with the gentle touch of her hand while Daddy played his guitar and sang, "You Are My Sunshine." Brother, whistling as usual, sprinted up the sidewalk, threw his schoolbooks on the front porch, and waved goodbye, fading as he floated away with Mother holding one hand and Daddy the other.

"No, don't go. Please. Talk to me. Say something. Please." If only I could hug them, touch them one more time. I couldn't hear their voices, but I could've sworn Mother said as she had so many times, "Remember, Gayle, you can do anything you set your mind to," and Brother again told me to, "Think, Gayle, think."

What if I'd listened to them and had set my mind to doing important work like environmental sciences. After all, I'd been worrying about our planet since I studied fossil fuels, long before I'd ever heard the words global warming, climate change, or recycle.

When my cousin Jenny and I were about six or seven and read about Johnny Appleseed, we set out to replenish the earth and not just with apple trees. For a few weeks, we saved every seed we could get our hands on. We even volunteered to throw out the watermelon rinds so we could collect the seeds. Mother couldn't believe it.

"You want to help clean up?" she said, with that suspicious tone in her voice and look in her eyes.

"You want to peel the peaches?"

"What in the world is going on?" she asked when I said I'd take out the trash so I could collect the rotten strawberries. Couldn't figure out how to get the tiny seeds off the outside so we decided to plant berries and all.

When we had two Mason jars full, we dug holes in our front and back yards, dumped the seeds in, and covered them up.

"You think we should've separated them?" Jenny asked as we tapped the dirt down on top of the last ones.

"You mean orange seeds in one hole and watermelons in another?"

"Yeah," she answered thoughtfully. "Maybe apple seeds don't like acorns."

"Oh well, too late now. Let's get started on the potatoes and carrots."

We scavenged Mother's kitchen, found four large bowls, filled each with one potato and one carrot, and poured water over them.

"We'll have to stick them in the closet," Jenny said, "so your mom won't see them and throw them out."

"When they grow those ugly root things, we'll plant them."

She nodded. "Won't our parents be surprised when the things start sprouting and they won't have to buy all that stuff at the store?"

Surprised was a mild word for what my parents were. Daddy fussed and carried on for at least three weeks, yelling about vandals and why would they do such a thing to his yard. He kept a clean, neat place, never bothered nobody. And if he ever found out who did it! He wasn't going to find out from me.

Mother kept walking around trying to figure out what that smell was and, finally, searched my room. Caught. She screamed something about a filthy mess and her missing bowls, yelled a few of Daddy's words and gagged as she threw our beautiful potatoes and carrots as hard and far as she could over the fence into the wooded vacant lot at the back of our property. They were at their perfect planting peak, too.

My parents' reactions were mild, though, compared to Aunt Teresa's when we tried to recycle the chickens. It was her fault. She shouldn't have taken us to visit Mama Lap and Papaw at chicken killing time. Those chickens were our friends. We'd named most of them, though it was hard to figure out which one was who.

Papaw chopped off their heads, and the poor little things jumped frantically around and around looking for them. After they collapsed, he dunked them in hot water and we had to pull the feathers off.

The cruelty and smell made us both mad and queasy. We kept sniffling and trying to figure out if he'd killed Mabel or Clyde or Buttercup and vowed never to eat chicken at Mama Lap and Papaw's house again. We preferred the kind of chicken Aunt Teresa and Mother bought that came from the store wrapped up and not alive.

So we could remember our poor departed friends, Jenny and I sneaked four of the chicken feet and buried them at the bottoms of our suitcases, to be given a proper funeral and reburied in our back yards.

All was well until we got home and Aunt Teresa opened our suitcases. Just like Mother, she gagged and shrieked and shouted Daddy's words and how could we do that to her and her brand new suitcases. She tossed our clothes out the window.

"What're you doing?" Jenny wailed.

Aunt Teresa wheezed and gasped, and we made out the words, "Burn them. Smell too bad. What in the world were you thinking?"

Neither of us had the courage to beg for our favorite shorts or shirts. But we cried for our chicken friends.

Slowly, I repacked the box holding the memories of my childhood and opened the next one. It contained baby clothes. On top was the pink frilly dress my firstborn, Diana, had looked so cute in, but she cried every time I tried to put it on her, so, I had packed it away in case I had another girl someday, but she cried too. The dress was still in perfect condition. Like my children.

In my eyes and heart every one of my four children was, and is, like Mary Poppins, practically-perfect-in-every-way. Of course, each one has his or her own ever so small flaws and idiosyncrasies.

Diana, for example, is always late. She was three weeks overdue before she decided to leave her quiet, peaceful existence inside my womb to enter this noisy, tumultuous world, and then she kicked, squirmed, pushed, shoved, and took her own sweet time making her entrance.

All the way to the hospital and for hours after I got there, I prayed, "Dear God, please get me out of this. I promise I won't do it again. I can't go through this. Please, God, please."

He not only didn't get me out of it, He sent me to a labor room nurse who'd obviously been trained as a Marine sergeant and looked like one. Stout. Big shoulders and face. Arms as muscular as Charles Atlas. No pleasantries passed between us.

I was so young. More scared than I'd ever been. And it didn't help any that the woman in the other bed, her hair wet and stringy, her face red and dripping with sweat, let out a blood-curdling scream like I'd heard only in movies just before the heroine was attacked by an alien monster. Then she glared at me with eyes that shrieked "Help!" I started for the door. I wanted my mother.

"Get out of those clothes," Sgt. No-compassion barked.

I took off everything except my panties to preserve my modesty, slipped into that gorgeous, fashionable hospital gown, sat on the other bed, and waited while Sarge read a bunch of papers, marking on them as intensely as an angry schoolteacher.

"Those, too."

"Huh…"

"Look, honey, they ain't figured out a way yet to give birth while wearing panties," Sarge growled in her superior-to-underling-who's-done-something-bad tone of voice.

Diana must've heard her being mean to her mommy. She kicked and pushed, and a contraction that felt like an iron snake clamped around my lower abdomen. I couldn't help it. When the nurse's arm came across in front of me, I bit it. And I wasn't sorry.

She screamed. No, I think it was me that screamed.

Twenty-four hours later when she presented me with Diana, my beautiful baby girl, all pain was forgotten. I learned the meaning of true love and forgot my vow to never do it again. I did it three more times.

As I repacked the box with baby clothes in it and placed it next to the one containing my childhood memories, words and scenes formed in my mind and compelled me to run to the back porch and start writing. This time the pen glided across the paper, and stories, especially the ones about my own childhood, poured onto the pages. I could almost see the house on Greenwood Street, where I spent the first seven or eight years of my life, its two front doors, and the swing on the porch. When I closed my eyes, I could see Brother and his friends playing baseball in the vacant lot, while my best friend and I played hopscotch on the sidewalk.

When my fingers stopped moving and I looked up at the sun, halfway through its afternoon descent, I had written at least eight pages of a short story entitled *The Yankees are Coming! The Yankees are Coming!* It was about the time I had paid a dime to the girl who lived down the street so I could watch Yankees walk from their car to the house.

THE YANKEES ARE COMING!
THE YANKEES ARE COMING!

It was August, 1949. Roy Rogers was King of the Cowboys; Tarzan wore a diaper, yelped like a sick dog, and swung through trees; Superman leapt tall buildings with a single bound, and I was the smartest girl about to enter second grade. I knew things other kids didn't, about that hat-seller guy, Harry, being president and folks with those ugly wire things on their roof having something called television. I figured television must be some kind of dreaded disease, like polio, and Cindy Lou McCallister had it. The only wire thing on the whole block was on top of her house, but that wasn't the only reason I didn't go near her.

She spied on me and my best friend, Calera, and every time we did anything wrong, like sneak off to the rock quarry or tie her little brother to a tree, she told on us. Sometimes she even told on us for things we didn't do. That's why I didn't believe her the day she said her daddy was going to the airport to pick up some Yankees.

It was a hot, summer afternoon, and me and Calera were minding our own business, playing paper dolls in the front yard, when who should come prissing down the sidewalk toward us?

Cindy Lou stopped two inches from my new Veronica and kicked grass and dirt on her green paper dress. "Hi, Gayle. Hi, Cal. Whatcha doing?"

We ignored her.

"I got a new doll." She opened the pink blanket cuddled in her arms and unveiled a baby doll wearing a pink and white dress, complete with matching cap, booties, and sweater. As she slowly turned the doll over, she smiled like she was a witch about to eat a poor, innocent girl. The doll cried, "Mama."

"So what?" Cal said. "I'd rather play with Betty and Veronica." She pointed to the book with its pages of clothes with tiny white tabs to hold them onto the cardboard teenagers.

But I wanted Cindy Lou's doll. It was just like the one I'd begged for but Mama said we couldn't afford. And how come she got a new toy when it wasn't even Christmas? Life wasn't fair.

"Yeah, who wants a baby that cries?" I said.

"Guess you don't want to see the Yankees either?"

"What Yankees?" Calera squinted as she looked up toward her majesty, the queen of snobbery and annoyance.

"The ones coming to my house tonight. Daddy's going to the airport to get them."

Cal and I jumped up, hands on our hips, eyes narrowed to show we didn't believe her.

"I can prove it," Cindy Lou said. "But it'll cost you a dime and you have to be in my yard tonight at eight."

"If I believed you, I'd be there," I said.

"You mean if your mama and daddy would let you out of the house. You're such a baby."

It was true. My parents would never let me out of the house after dark, but no way would I admit it. "I'll be there."

"But, Gayle, don't you remember what your granny said?" Cal put her hands over her mouth, leaned over, and whispered. Her warm breath tickled my ear. "She said those damn Yankees are evil and start fights and tell stories."

"Scaredy cats." Cindy Lou stuck her tongue out.

"Are not."

"Are too."

"Are not."

"You're scared of the Yankees. Bet you never seen one."

"Neither have you." I wanted to punch her two big front teeth out.

"I will tonight." Her mouth twisted into one of her witch smiles. "Tell you what. If you don't see them Yankees tonight, I'll give you my doll."

Calera yelled, "We don't want your ugly old doll."

"Now, hold on a minute, Cal." I grabbed Cindy Lou's hand and shook it.

"And what if you lose, what do I get?" Cindy Lou's green eyes glinted in the sunshine like our cat's when he got ready to pounce on a poor, defenseless chipmunk, and she was so tall I had to look up at her. "I know. You can do my homework for a week."

"No way."

"Then you admit the Yankees are coming."

Visions of holding, dressing, and rocking that doll flashed through my mind. I dug into my pocket, pulled out my ice cream money, threw my dime at her witchiness, and punched Cal in the arm until she did the same.

"Hide in the bushes and keep your mouth shut, you hear?" Her red and blonde streaked curls frizzed and tumbled over each other like her head was on fire, and sweat trickled down her face into the corners of her mouth. She licked it off.

Cindy Lou had to be from outer space, some place where girls grew big and mean. Not Krypton, though. She was nothing like Superman. "You're one of 'them,' aren't you?"

Cindy Lou balled her hand into a huge fist and drew it back like a baseball pitcher about to deliver his fast one, but she didn't scare me none. I ran because Cal grabbed my hand, took off running, and just about jerked my arm loose from my body.

"My mama ain't going to let me go." Cal dropped onto the ground under the apple tree in my back yard, pushed her hair from her face, tried to wipe the sweat from her skin, and left a trail of moist dirt on her forehead and temples.

I plopped down beside her, my knees bent, my hands behind my head, and one foot propped on the other. The grass, dry and brown from the hot August sun, tickled my back where my shorts and shirt parted. "Don't you want to know what they're like?"

"Sure," Cal said. "But—" She stopped, and I knew she was trying to make up some excuse not to go. Mama said Cal and I were so alike we even knew what the other one was thinking. And we looked alike, too, pale skin that blotched and reddened in sunshine, both of us almost eight years old, blue eyes. I had freckles and light brown hair that streaked with blonde in the summer. Hers was the color of corn silks all year round.

"You got to go with me," I said. "It's our duty. Granny told us those damned Yankees came here before and beat up on us and wouldn't leave till they recon—re—reconstrued us. Folks didn't have enough to eat, and they was fighting and everything."

"Nope, not a chance. Last time we done our duty I got a spanking and was grounded for two weeks."

"What if they're big and mean and ugly and want to fight your daddy and steal his money?"

She shook her head.

"We got to be brave, Cal." I sat up and placed my hand over my heart, like we did in school when we said the Pledge of 'Legiance. "The whole world needs us."

"No way. No. I won't do it."

"You know that huge tree in Cindy Lou's yard? We'll get some fishing line from your dad's stuff, tie it around the tree real close to the ground so they won't see it, and tie the other end around the dogwood on the other side of the walk."

"And they'll trip and skin their knees. That's real smart. If they don't kill us, my daddy will."

I ignored her. "We'll get the badminton net from our back yard, and when they fall, we'll throw it over them, tie 'em up and call the police."

"Oh, alright, maybe it'll work."

We spent the rest of the afternoon stealing the badminton net and the fishing line and tying the line to the tree. When Mama hollered out the back door that dinner was ready, Cal pointed her finger in my face just like Mama did when she was mad at me. "I'll meet you at the crape myrtle at 8:00. You better be there."

All during dinner, my heart thudded. My stomach gurgled and sputtered, and I couldn't eat a thing. All I wanted was for Mama and Daddy to hurry up and eat their food so I could save them from those Yankees. But no, they ate so slow a turtle could've eaten quicker.

Suddenly, Mama glanced at my plate. "Gayle, you haven't eaten a thing."

"May I be excused, please?" I asked as politely as I could.

"No," Mama answered. "Eat your dinner."

So, while my parents yapped some more, I pushed my potatoes around, stuffed collard greens under the plate, and gave my chicken leg to Bubbles, our cocker spaniel. I was just about to ask if I could go outside when Mama saw the dog gnawing the bone and screeched, grabbed the bone, and yelled something about me eating and the dog getting choked and told me I couldn't have dessert.

Finally, when I'd given up hope of ever getting through dinner, Daddy pushed his chair from the table. "You know, I read today that more murders are committed in August than any other time of the year." He paused and waited for Mama to answer, but she was busy collecting bowls and plates from the table. "Seems all this heat and humidity makes folks right testy."

"I've thought about it a few times myself," Mama said, tugging at her red plaid shirt, trying to pry it loose from her damp skin.

Good grief. If Mama thought about murder, what would the Yankees do?

"Guess I'll go outside where it's a bit cooler," Daddy said. He trudged to the front porch, wiping sweat from his face and mumbling words I didn't understand. I followed, determined to ask him what Yankees were like and could I go see them. He settled into his rocker and unfolded the newspaper. The sun's last rays of the day peeked through the trees and settled across our front porch while the lingering aroma of Mama's fried chicken and biscuits filled the air. A warm wind blew through the paper. He clutched its edges. The sports section fluttered to the floor. He bellowed a word he'd spanked me for saying and kicked a pot of geraniums. Best not to bother him.

If he found out what I was about to do, he wouldn't understand, and I'd probably be sent to my room until high school graduation, but I had to do it. It was my duty, and I wasn't a bit scared. It was close to 8:00 when I finally got to my room and, pretending it was Superman's cape, tied a towel around my neck, climbed out my window onto the garage roof, jumped to the ground, and raced to the crape myrtle.

Cal was waiting and mad. "Where've you been? Them Yankees probably already beat up Cindy Lou."

"No, she's one of them." I galloped right by her, and she fell in step beside me. With the cape flapping around my shoulder, I was off to save the world.

So was the rest of the neighborhood. At least a dozen kids tromped around Cindy Lou's yard. Big mean Lester, the third-grade bully, trampled Mrs. McCallister's begonias and bragged about what he was going to do to the Yankees. A couple of the girls practiced cartwheels while Gopher Harris laughed and punched Fred Jr. in the shoulder. Others shouted stuff like, "Where's the Yankees?" and, "They better get here in a hurry, Cindy Lou, or we're going to make mincemeat out of you."

Cindy Lou stood on the front porch, her big front teeth flashed, and her fiery hair danced in the yellow of the porch light. "Y'all be quiet now!" she shouted, "and hide in the bushes so Daddy won't see you."

Nobody paid any attention to her until a black Chevrolet pulled up and parked in the driveway and she screamed, "Hide! Hide!"

Suddenly, it got so quiet I could hear the crickets and tree frogs chirping. My heart pounded, and Calera caught her breath and held it so long I had to hit her in the back to make her let it go. She clutched one end of the badminton net while I held on to the other.

Mr. McCallister stepped from the car and scanned the crowd for the longest time. His eyes blazed as he glared into Lester's face, at one of the cartwheel girls, and at me. He must be the ringleader, I thought, and he's going to take us prisoner and do bad things to us. Finally, he yelled, "Get out of here, all of you!"

But I wasn't about to go anywhere, at least not until I saw them Yankees. Nobody else moved either.

Mr. McCallister, as slow as cold molasses, walked around the car and opened the door for a tall, round woman who stuck her nose in the air the same way Cindy Lou always did and marched toward the house.

A little boy about my age, holding onto the woman's skirt, stuck his tongue out at me as he pranced by. I reached out and touched his ear and face, as soft and warm as mine and Calera's, and punched his upper arm. That little devil kicked my leg, ran behind Mr. McCallister, peeked around, and smiled and winked at me.

The woman sniffed at the sky, grasped the boy's hand, took two steps forward, and screamed like a wounded opera singer as she tumbled forward and landed on the concrete, hands and huge breasts first.

"Where's the Yankees, you fraud?" someone yelled.

"Wait'll I get my hands on you." Lester doubled one fist and, right in Cindy Lou's face, smacked it into the palm of his other hand.

Gopher pushed Fred Jr., and everybody started hitting and saying stuff they weren't supposed to, while Mr. McCallister roared and threatened to call the police and tell all the parents what rotten children they were raising.

"Those are the Yankees?" Still holding onto the net, Cal and I raced over to the car and searched inside. "I want my money back," I yelled. "They're just like us."

Something strong and hard clamped itself on my shoulder. I turned and saw the woman, who had somehow managed to get her huge self up and off the sidewalk, towering over us, her face scratched and bleeding. At the same time, Cal and I dropped the net and, as fast as our legs would go, dashed home, collapsed in the front yard, and gazed, silently, at the full moon and stars while lightning bugs flew around us. I slapped at the mosquitoes trying to eat my leg, and Cal scratched her arms. Bubbles licked me in the face.

Finally, Cal whispered, "Maybe we shouldn't have tied that fishing line between those trees."

"I touched him," I whispered too, even though nobody was around but us.

"That Yankee boy?"

I nodded and rubbed the red place on my shin. "Wonder if he'd like to play Superman and jump off the garage with us tomorrow?"

"Yeah, we could save the world from Cindy Lou and that wire-on-the-roof disease."

"And he might sneak her baby doll out so I could play with it—just for a little while."

five

A WHOLE NOTEBOOK FULL

A few days later I'd written a whole notebook full of stories about my childhood, my children, and grandchildren. Maybe I could put it all together in a book and give it to them for Christmas. I could include pictures, too, not just those stiff, posed ones, but also the funny ones.

Someday, Catherine Lee, Mark, and Carly could read stories about their great-great-grandmothers and look at pictures of them. Mama Lap trying to hide behind her apron because her hair was frizzy that day. Grandmother picking flowers around my grandfather's grave. They could explain to their children that my stepfather, great-grandfather Pawpaw, was wearing a red dress because he, along with the male doctors at Medical Center East, was in a womanless wedding.

That, yes, great-grandmother Mawmaw, laughed a lot and their great-uncle Buddy, my brother, often smiled as if he knew some mischievous something that might embarrass me, and he just might tell it. They could read stories about their mom and dad and Aunt Diana and Uncle Darrin as children and point out pictures of them on their bicycles or unwrapping Christmas presents in the midst of a mountain of paper and bows, boxes and toys.

Sitting there that day, reading over the stories in my notebook, I realized how different each of my children were from each other and from me. No one would guess we had all lived together for so many years.

Diana was always the skeptic. One Christmas Eve, when she was five, I was on my way to bed at about 1:00 a.m. when I heard a slight noise from her room. I peeked in to find her staring out the window. "Diana, honey, what are you doing?" I asked gently. "How can Santa come see you if you aren't asleep?"

"But, Mommy, I just don't understand how one man can see all the little children in the world. I want to see if he's real."

She was also stubborn.

She was still a toddler the day she picked up my grandmother's dinner bell. "No, we don't touch that," I said, kindly and gently, pulling her away from the table and trying to divert her attention.

She clamped her hand around that bell and stared me in the eyes as if to say, "You gonna make me?" She rang the bell defiantly and then, on her way to her room, threw a tantrum worthy of a diva.

When Diana was eighteen months old, her little brother, Darrin, was born. She liked to hit him, so I handed her a brand new baby doll that resembled a newborn and calmly said, "When you feel like hitting your little brother, punch this doll instead." A few minutes later I caught her whamming that doll against the wall over and over as hard as she could.

Darrin was different from his older sister.

Later I had the same bell confrontation with him. Like I did with Diana, I said, "We don't play with this bell; it's special to Mawmaw." Darrin looked up at me with his big, innocent blue eyes, smiled, put it down, and picked up a toy. A few minutes later I heard a clank. He had the bell turned upside down, and his little fingers were exploring its underside, trying to take it apart.

Another characteristic peculiar to Darrin was that he liked to buy stuff—immediately upon arriving somewhere. One time at an amusement park, he saw a giant sombrero; immediately, he knew he wanted that hat more than anything in the world. I told him we would get it on the way out, so we wouldn't have to carry it all day, but he worried, whined, and carried on for so long that, finally, in sheer desperation, I bought the sombrero. We took it on the Ferris wheel ("Mom! You're smushing it!"), held on frantically as it flapped about on the Tilt-a-Whirl ("Mom! Don't let goooooo!"), and protected it on the bumper cars ("Mom! Don't let Diana touch it!"), and then he wore it in our Volkswagen on the way home so that all I could see in the rearview mirror was the cone of that sombrero. But my son was all smiles because he had his hat.

It was the same at the grocery store. The minute I set him in the child seat of the cart, he started crying. He wanted candy, cereal, toys, everything. One day, when he was about three, he hollered and carried on all the way through the store. I ignored him. People watched to see what I would do. I mentally counted the money in my billfold, bargaining with myself, but no matter how I worked it, we couldn't afford a treat for him, so I told him he couldn't have anything. He screamed louder.

Finally, an angry masculine voice came over the loud speaker, "Darrin." A pause. Another "DARRIN."

My Darrin got still and quiet. He looked around, down and up at the ceiling, his eyes filled with fear, but he didn't make another sound the rest of the shopping trip.

Like Diana, Darrin wasn't happy about the arrival of a baby. "How come we got her?" he asked when I brought Cathy home from the hospital.

"Because I prayed for a little sister," seven-year-old Diana answered, and forever after she thought of Cathy as her little girl.

They'd sit for hours playing school, Diana the teacher, Cathy the ever-willing and easily-taught student. It didn't bother her that her older sister locked her in a room and wouldn't let her out until she correctly completed her spelling or reading "homework." Math was her specialty, and at two, she could play Yahtzee and was able to identify a flush, a straight, or a full house without any help.

One time when she was five, I handed my money to the cashier at the McDonald's and, when she gave me the change, Cathy said, "That's not right."

"What's not right?"

"The change. She owes you another dime."

I counted, and she was right.

Cathy was also the experimenter. Once, when she was about two or three, she asked if she could fix eggs. I was on the phone at the time and thought she meant pretend cook. I told her, "Sure." When I got off the phone and went into the kitchen, she had every pot and pan I owned on the floor, eggs cracked into all of them and all over the floor, shells and all. Over this she'd spread a whole jar of unpopped popcorn. I started to say something stern but could only laugh. After all, she'd asked.

Like Darrin before her, Cathy wasn't entirely enchanted when a new baby was born—but the rest of us were. Scott was the baby, and everything he did was cute and funny to all of us—for a while. Cathy and Darrin quickly focused their attention from him back to their childhood activities, but Diana became his second mom. She sang to him, talked to him, and taught him things more gently than she had Cathy. And her friends loved Scott. They giggled and laughed and fawned over him, and he loved it.

He couldn't have been more than eighteen months when he was learning the parts of the body. I sat on the couch with him in my lap to watch television and a beautiful, very buxom woman appeared on the screen and started singing.

Scott's little eyes were riveted on her as he exclaimed, "Wow, she's got elbows." (He still likes "elbows").

The one thing Scott hated most in the world was getting up early in the morning, and often, after I woke him, he'd hide. One morning when he was about four or five and I was desperate to get my children fed, dressed, and out the door so they wouldn't miss their school bus and I wouldn't be late for work, we couldn't find him. Diana, Darrin, Cathy, and I split up for the search. Not in his room. Or the bathroom. Not in the kitchen. There was, however, a full bowl of soggy mini-wheats at his place at the table.

Suddenly, we heard a whooshing sound. At the same time, we heard a screech and a shout, just as the door to the coat closet burst open and Scott tumbled out in the midst of a sea of white foam. We're still laughing, and he still has a healthy respect for fire extinguishers.

When I finished reading the notebook, I took it to the computer to transcribe its contents into a Word document, and, hopefully, create a memorable Christmas present for my children. That's when I remembered two poems I'd written years before. Back to the boxes. It took a while but I found them, and I inserted them in my memoir.

SON

I look into his face and I can see
Infant eyes smiling at me,
As his bicycle spins, he drives a car,
Reads Dr. Seuss, studies planets and stars.

Gathering dandelions and flowers for Mom,
He pins a white orchid on his date for the prom,
He jumps from his cradle and gives Mom a hug,
Handsome and strong, he plays with a bug.

He climbs a tree, chases a squirrel,
Throws the softball and catches a girl,
Watching spiders, playing with a frog,
Blond curls bouncing, he's off to a job.

Though the cradle is empty, I can't stop rocking,
Soothing skinned knees, filling the stocking.
I turn him loose, he'll go anyway,
He was only mine for a short summer's day.

I look into their faces and I can see
His infant eyes smiling at me,
They ride their tricycles, chase a squirrel,
Dandelions for Nana, They're Daddy's "big boy and girl."

Laundry's piled high now, dinner's late,
Together we catch fireflies, dig for bait,
Through fields and flowers we gleefully roam,
Squealing and laughing—before this summer's gone.

DAUGHTER

Barbie sits on her plastic couch in her plastic house and waits to be changed from her red velvet gown into tiny summer shorts, for her pale pink telephone to ring, or maybe for a visit from Ken. But the two giggly goddesses who controlled her world, had one day shut her in the closet and never came back.

Occasionally she thinks she hears their voices on the other side of the door, but they're different now, more grown up, and there are no giggles, no laughter, no fun, no playing. Still she waits. Remembers. Cries nostalgic tears.

Until one day the door flings open. Light rushes in. Small hands snatch her up, hug her, and pull her hair.

This new little goddess squeals and giggles while Barbie's two goddesses, the ones she always loved, laugh and giggle and tug at her dress, and their large fingers fumble through Barbie's many outfits.

six

A NOVEL, GRANDCHILDREN,
AND BEACH TRAFFIC—IN THAT ORDER

A couple of weeks later, while sipping coffee, listening to the birds, and watching the roses bloom, I reread the first chapter of the novel I'd retrieved from its resting place in a file marked "personal." I'd started it years ago during my divorce proceedings and worked on it from time to time, usually when I was angry at someone I loved. Maybe it had some interesting insights I could include in the book I was writing for my children.

Though I'd crossed out the scene where I tied my ex-husband to a tree and set it on fire and the one where he accidently fell on his own gun and it went off, my fury showed. As did the anxiety, distress, and absolute misery that accompany the failure and defeat of divorce. In my novice voice, however, this novel was not a viable or publishable story, though it had been therapeutic for me to write.

I wondered. With my now 20/20 hindsight, could I turn this into a sellable novel? Of course I could. All I had to do was type this manuscript into a brand new Word document, changing words, sentences, and paragraphs as I went. I'd work on my novel in the morning, my memoir at night. By this time next year, I could have two manuscripts finished.

Without stopping at the refrigerator or pantry, I went straight to the computer and started typing. Joy of joys, thoughts and ideas flowed. When Heather, my heroine, cried, I cried; when she laughed, so did I.

I was there with her when her husband threatened her and she ran from the house, through the neighbors' yards, down the street. I felt the cold biting her lips and nose and saw the overcast sky and black snow at the edges of the frozen street. I felt the contraction in her abdomen when the baby kicked, and I smelled the smoke from the chimney of the brick, ranch-style house on the corner.

That's when the doorbell rang, and I suddenly remembered that Catherine Lee and Mark were home from summer camp and were going to spend the remainder of their summer days with me. Quickly, I saved my embryo novel and sprinted to the front door.

I knew this precious time with my grandchildren was limited and, like their dad, they'd too soon be grown. We had a great vacation planned. We were going to visit their Aunt Cathy and cousin Carly in Nashville and then their Aunt Diana in Monroeville, Alabama. Like they say, grandchildren are God's gift to parents who don't strangle their young. A second chance. Joy without responsibility.

It was also a great time to expand my writing and work from a different environment. Every night I'd record the day's highlights and how I felt about each event. I'd ask Catherine Lee, then thirteen, and Mark, twelve, for insight into how they felt and what they learned, and I'd talk to little Carly, my very expressive three-year-old granddaughter. I'd take time to listen to their thoughts and feelings, so I could understand them better and appreciate their uniqueness.

Yep, it was going to be grand. I couldn't wait.

One grandmother, two grandchildren, together 24/7 for two weeks, a lot of the time traveling north and south on I-65. The memory reminds me of those video games they play, only I'm the one who gets shot down and, amazingly, pops right back up to get shot again. And again.

The first day on the way to Nashville we were happily moving along on I-65, me listening to Elvis, them in the back seat watching a movie, the sun shining brightly. All was right with my world. My heroine whispered in my ear; she was ready to get even with Walter for leaving her for another woman, and she knew just how to do it. Suddenly, the DVD clicked off. No, the back-seat movie couldn't be over. Not yet. I was having too good a time with my heroine.

"I'm not watching that," Catherine Lee said.

"You picked the last one."

"That didn't count. You wanted to watch it too."

"It does count."

"We're watching this one."

"No, we're not."

Scuffling noises. Car rocking.

"Ouch, that hurt."

"You're such a baby."

"Yeah, you wanna see how it feels?"

More wrestling. I started looking for an exit with a McDonald's. They needed totally unhealthy, coma-producing junk food, like a hamburger, fries, milkshake, and cookies. I needed a tranquilizer. When they were younger, they'd been easier. They usually slept on road trips. Then there was the time when they were about three and four, and all the way from Nashville to Birmingham, they made up songs about poop, but at least they did it together, laughing all the way. Now, the moments of togetherness were few and far between.

At McDonald's, they were too old for the playground and too young to sit still, but just the right age for arguing, jostling, and annoying Nana. When we left and while I merged with the traffic on I-65, they restarted their argument about which movie to watch. Just as I was ready to jump out of the car, both of them dozed off. Quiet. Peace. Elvis and I sang together, restoring my wits and sanity, and it occurred to me—I know this sounds crazy—it occurred to me that I loved this trip, even the arguing. In a few short years, like their dad, they'd be grown, and I'd long for this day and this time with them.

For a few minutes, Catherine Lee was a toddler again, hovering over her baby brother, jerking the pacifier from his mouth to hers and when he cried, soothing him like a mommy. Her first complete sentence had been, "Where's my Mark?" They fought, rolling on the floor, screaming and crying. But when Mark was hurt, Catherine Lee was the first one there, finding what hurt him and drying his tears.

Catherine Lee, almost from birth, was supremely organized and efficient, just like her mother. I could explain how to do something one time and she listened and grasped it. Even when she was a child, possibly as young as seven, I occasionally on weekends hired her to dust and vacuum for me to give her extra money, and she always did a good job. When she was about thirteen, she reorganized my kitchen for me. Small appliances together on one end of the shelf. The silverware drawer should be the one closest to the dishwasher.

Mark is organized like I'm organized—that is to say, not at all. If you asked him to go to the kitchen to get a glass of water, he'd stop to talk to the dog and see an interesting plant, which he'd then stop to examine. In examining the plant, he'd find a toy car he hadn't seen in a while, and he'd pick it up to play with it. As he played with the car, he'd think, "What was that song we heard yesterday?" and run back to ask me. When I asked him about the original glass of water, he'd simply stare at me blankly like I'd lost my mind.

Both children are amazingly imaginative. Catherine Lee and her friend Taylor made up games, organized their friends, and told them how to play. Mark liked to put assorted items in the freezer to see what would happen. One time I opened the freezer door and screamed when I found a dead spider in an ice cube. They spent an entire summer playing with boiled eggs, dressing them in paper napkins they'd decorated with crayons, scraps of paper, and strings, and then hiding them. I'm not sure what else they did to them, but it entertained them and kept them quiet, so I kept buying and boiling eggs.

Those days were gone. They were about to step onto the precipice between childhood and adulthood, and head down that road that their dad, uncle, and aunts had perilously and not so long ago raced through, leaving me an exhausted, sniveling "space cadet." My children's nomenclature, not mine.

How could I let them go too? How could I stop them? My mind knew and understood that they would grow up, and I would proudly sniff and cry when they walked across the stage to accept their degrees, when they married, and, especially, when I held my first great-grandchild. But forever in my heart, they are, and will always be, my babies.

Thank goodness Carly was still my baby. When we arrived at her house in Nashville, she'd run out to meet me, smiling, her arms open, shouting, "Nana! Nana!" and jump into my arms, just like Catherine Lee and Mark used to do. She'd let me push her in the swing, show me her newest collection of bugs, and together we'd make an inedible concoction of flour, sugar, oatmeal, salt, and whatever else we could find. And that's exactly what happened that day.

Being with my daughter Cathy and my grandchildren was just what I needed. I felt energized and ready to have fun. After the children were in bed that night and while Cathy played games on her computer, I pulled out my notebook and recorded the events of the day.

The next day Cathy and I decided to take Catherine Lee, Mark, and Carly to the water park. Great. What fun. We couldn't wait. It was the first and only swimming pool I ever went to where they searched my purse before taking my money.

"You can't take those in," the cute young thing in the tight, bright red t-shirt said.

"They're juice boxes for my granddaughter," I said, pointing to three-year-old Carly.

"You can't take them in."

"I'm taking them in."

"You have to buy drinks inside."

"Are there any healthy drinks inside?"

"Coca-Cola, Pepsi..." said Miss Stuffed Shirt.

Cathy, who limited Carly's sugar intake and tried diligently to keep her diet as healthy as possible, was getting a tiny bit miffed. "Do you have milk? Real fruit juice? You have heard of them, haven't you?"

"How would I know, lady? I just work here."

"I want to see your manager," Cathy said.

By this time Catherine Lee and Mark had moved away from us and acted like they didn't know us.

In her stroller, with tiny drops of sweat on her beautiful little face, Carly wiped at her forehead with one hand and cried out, "I'm thirsty!"

She'd started saying words when she was about six months and by age one could carry on a conversation—or at least she tried to—but sometimes other methods got more attention and she wasn't afraid to use them. She unfastened the safety belt, climbed out of the stroller, stood with her hands on her hips, glared at the attendant, and spewed out a long sequence of words that conveyed annoyance even if we only understood a few of them, like "mad," "hot," and "home."

Miss Employee-Guard-of-the-Day stood in front of the entrance. "I can't leave my post."

Cathy didn't budge. A long line of hot, angry people was inching their way toward us.

"I'm not leaving until you get the manager."

I could feel the sunshine burning my face, and the perspiration plastering my bangs to my forehead. My t-shirt was damp.

"You're not going in with those boxes of juice." Her guardship put her hands on her hips.

Finally, I tugged at Cathy's arm and suggested, "Let's just give her some juice now."

We made a big production of moving our beach bags and Carly to a nearby bench, which was not in the shade. Cathy whipped out an apple juice, poured it into Carly's cup, snapped it shut, and handed it to her. I stuffed two more boxes into the waist band of my shorts and covered them with my baggy t-shirt.

Then I sauntered innocently past the guard without incident, with Catherine Lee and Mark trailing far enough behind us that no one would know they came with us. Her Highness, the royal keeper of the gate, stepped aside as Cathy pushed Carly through the gate.

Except for a few mishaps and a couple of arguments, the rest of the week was a piece of cake. After the children were in bed at night, Cathy and I talked about and solved all kinds of problems, both personal and political. As we'd done many times before, we shared our opinions on everything from what each family member was up to and what they should be doing to how to balance the federal budget. Each night I faithfully wrote something in my notebook.

On to Monroeville and Aunt Diana.

Monroeville's claim to fame is that it's where Harper Lee grew up and Truman Capote spent his summers with his aunt. Its main tourist attraction is Harper Lee and the famous courthouse where her father, aka Atticus Finch, once practiced. *To Kill a Mockingbird* was still enacted every year at the Old Monroe County Courthouse. In my mind, however, the main attraction was the local community college's stellar English instructor, who also happened to be my daughter, Diana.

I was sure Catherine Lee and Mark would jump at the chance to visit a few of her classes and take advantage of this opportunity to experience the joys of higher learning.

Not so much.

Though my daughter's classroom was so cold I shivered, and my hands were numb and it was right before lunch and my stomach growled, I felt like a kid again on the first day of a new school year, but in a different time zone, a different universe. Maybe where the Jetsons lived.

I've always considered myself reasonably intelligent, able to learn new things and adapt, but I must confess today's technology has passed me by. iPods, Wii, phones that take pictures? When I was in school, blackboards were, well, black, and the teacher wrote on them with chalk with her back to the class. Still, she always knew who spit the tiny, wadded-up, paper ball and who passed the note. Now that was high tech. When my children were in school, the blackboards were green. In Diana's world the blackboards were white, and they weren't even blackboards. They were Smartboards. While she sat at her desk and moved her fingers, words appeared on the whiteboard.

Catherine Lee and Mark were drawn to the thing like hungry children in a car to big yellow arches, and their hands started slapping at it as they both shouted, "I got it first!" Just as I was about to grab their hands and pull them away from what surely cost thousands of dollars that I'd be responsible for paying when they broke it, Diana handed each of them a handful of papers.

"Please place one on each desk," she asked calmly and politely.

They both ran for the same desk. "You go that way!" Mark shouted, pointing to the other side of the room.

Instead, Catherine Lee tried to put her paper down on that particular desk, and Mark tried to push her away. They chased each other up and down the aisles, pushing, shoving, and laughing hysterically. At the same time the students, also laughing and talking and making noise, filed into the room and were greeted by these two preteens in a game of "slap the desk with paper" and "catch me if you can." One young man caught his paper as it flew toward his face, and another picked his off the floor and dusted off the footprint.

Now everyone who knows me knows that chaos shatters my nerves and freezes my brain. I was about to jump up, scream, and tell them all to sit down and shut up when a miracle happened. Diana slowly and calmly walked to the door, closed it, and walked back to her desk. As she played with the thing on her desk and made words appear on the board, the entire class, including Catherine Lee and Mark, sat at attention, waiting for her to speak. Which she did. About Shakespeare and Hamlet.

I was fascinated with her intelligent and insightful questions, "How would you describe Hamlet's relationship with Gertrude? Is Hamlet's uncle really his father's murderer? Is Hamlet insane?" Some of the kids actually raised their hands and discussed their ideas, especially the insanity issue. Diana had to be the best teacher in the world. I was sure Catherine Lee and Mark shared my enthusiasm, until I glanced their way to be sure.

Mark was eyeing the red-headed girl in the front row, the one wearing a tight, white sleeveless shirt that ended just above her belly button. Catherine Lee was doodling in her notebook.

Diana moved to the front of her desk and leaned back against it as she asked, "What is Hamlet's flaw that causes his downfall?"

Catherine Lee, softly and quietly, crept to Diana's desk and sat down. Mark followed her. Diana kept on talking. Suddenly, words, childish pictures, and lines that had nothing to do with Shakespeare or Hamlet appeared on the board behind her. "Mark is weird." "Catherine Lee likes Lyle." A heart. A car. A spaceship.

When Diana asked the class, "How does Shakespeare seem to view insanity based on these characters?" the students giggled in anticipation, like kids hiding behind a bush waiting to jump out at their victim. Diana's expression immediately changed from pleasant to school-teacher annoyance. She stopped talking. Her head turned ever so slightly to the right and her eyes stared at her niece and nephew. The class got quiet; Catherine Lee and Mark froze. Those few quiet moments seemed like an hour.

Finally, Diana said, "Sit. Down. Now." When they had complied, she turned and repeated her question to the class.

How Mark did it I don't know, but he fell out of his seat and landed with a bang on the floor. Suddenly, loud laughter filled the room. One girl jumped from her seat and tried to help him up. Others crowded around him to see what was happening while Catherine Lee laughed hysterically. Amid the chaos, I heard Diana's school-teacher voice command me to take my wayward grandchildren from her class—immediately. I rushed toward them and began shooing them to the exit. The students, still giggling, returned to their seats. For the third time, my daughter asked the same question.

One girl raised her hand and started talking, but I couldn't hear what she said. My mind was too busy outlining what torture I'd inflict on my two class clowns as punishment. On the ride home, I'd play Elvis so loud they couldn't hear their music. They wouldn't be allowed to use Diana's Wii the rest of our visit. We wouldn't stop at McDonald's for the next month.

Later, after chastising them repeatedly during the drive to Radley's Fountain Grill, Catherine Lee, Mark, and I sat at a table, waiting for Diana to join us for lunch. I'd almost forgotten about their crimes and my envisioned punishment, but as soon as I saw Diana enter the door and march toward us, I knew she hadn't. It was the walk of an angry schoolteacher. She sat down and stared at her errant niece and nephew but said nothing, which reminded me of my junior high history teacher, Mrs. Turner. Like her, my Diana, my baby-turned-grown up, had that same ability to be infuriated and composed at the same time and by saying nothing could instill fear into the hearts of adolescents. I didn't say anything either.

Finally, she asked, "Did you enjoy my class?"

"Yes, ma'am," Catherine Lee and Mark answered in unison.

Again, for a few minutes, she said nothing. The proverbial pregnant pause. Even I was uncomfortable, like I'd been in Mrs. Turner's class.

In her sternest schoolteacher voice, Diana said, "If you ever do that again, I won't be responsible for my actions."

After that, no one spoke until the waitress came over, whipped out her writing pad, and asked cheerfully, "Can I get y'all something to drink?"

Catherine Lee and Mark glanced at Diana to see if it was okay to order. She smiled. Everyone relaxed, and my daughter and grandchildren started talking about the cool Smartboard. When we attended her night class, however, they were the best-behaved kids in the room.

Leaving is always such sweet sorrow. On the morning of our planned departure, teary-eyed, I hugged Diana and told her we'd be gone when she got home.

"Be sure you have everything you need before you close the back door," she instructed. "It'll lock when you do."

We packed our suitcases and put them by the car, checked and double checked for everything we'd brought. Finally, I slammed the back door and groped through my purse for my car keys. Not there. Not on the back porch.

I called Diana. She was in the middle of a class and would come home as soon as possible. While waiting, we searched the driveway, grass, bushes and under the car. Now, South Alabama in August is hotter than the hinges of Hades, and the humidity is about ninety percent. I could feel my face burning. Sweat seeped out of my pores and created tiny, dribbling pools on my skin. Fatigue settled in my bones. And just on the other side of her door was cool, refreshing air conditioning.

Right before I passed out from heat exhaustion, like my rescuing guardian angel, Diana appeared, let us in, and helped me search for what seemed like hours. Those darn keys weren't on the dining room table where I usually left them. Nor the kitchen counter. Or the bedside table.

"Uh, have y'all seen my car keys?" I reluctantly asked Catherine Lee and Mark, who, by this time, had plopped on the couch and were playing a video game. They looked up at me incredulously.

Not yet panicked but getting antsy, I again ran to the car and tried to open the driver's side door. Locked. I peeked inside. No key in the ignition. "I had to have them to get here," I whined.

Diana had to go back to work, so I called a locksmith. He promised me he could not only open my car door but he could also make a key for me, but when he got there, all promises were off. Breaking into an Acura is evidently difficult and making a key for it is impossible.

"You'll have to get the keys from the dealer," he said.

"But there's no Acura dealer in Monroeville," I screeched. Now I was panicked, and I blamed him for my predicament. He should've been a better locksmith. I called Clay who had to overnight the extra Acura key to me.

We left the next day. The thing about traveling I-65 North through South Alabama in the summer is all that beach traffic. It was rush hour the whole way home. Bumper to bumper. Slow moving right lane. But I didn't dare get in the left lane.

From the backseat déjà vu:

"I'm not watching that."

"I'm not watching that."

"Give it to me."

"Shut up, Catherine Lee."

"You make me, Mark."

"I will."

Car rocking. Screams. Shouts. Scuffling noises. Where was that McDonald's exit? Car on my bumper.

"You idiot, I'm in the right lane. Go around me!" I yelled.

"He can't hear you, Nana."

"Dammit, I know that." Freaking truck passing on a hill. Car behind almost hit him. Interstate traffic slamming on brakes. This was not good.

"Then why did you yell?"

"I felt like it."

"That's stupid."

"Shut up."

"You don't have to yell at us."

I bit my arm. It bled. I cried. Traffic all around me blurred. At the hospital that night, the doctor said I hadn't had a heart attack, but my blood pressure was way up, and they would keep me overnight just in case.

Maybe two weeks was too long to be on the road with two high-spirited teenagers. Toward the end of our week with Diana, we were all tired and a bit cranky. She and I, like Cathy and me, had stayed up late to discuss all the problems of our family, the plight of our beleaguered planet, and the fate of the American educational system. By bedtime each night, I'd been so tired, I could only manage a couple of lines, and my handwriting had been so poor I couldn't read them the next morning. No great insight, inspiration, or novel came out of those exhausted ramblings, but at least of couple of poems survived my grandchildren's adventures.

THE ROBIN

I watch the robin,
Soaring and free,
And wonder if he, like me,
Longs to flee
The burning smog and

Oil-slicked sea,
Great Tributes to Man's Ingenuity.

THE STUDENT

Inside the well-manicured lawn
Grew blades of perfect grass,
Lush and green,
Each one as beautiful as the next.

In the midst of the grass
A dandelion blossomed and grew
Tall and strong,
And higher than the rest.

It swayed in the breeze,
Lighthearted and free,
Blowing its creative lightness
Across the Earth

Until the huge machine
Chopped off its head,
And seeing it not dead,
Reached down its hands to choke
The life out of it.

The hands tugged and pulled
And bruised the tiny flower
Until finally, in pain, it gave up,
Withered at its roots and allowed itself
To be thrown into the basket
With the castoffs.

But its seeds would not die.
And they spring forth still
In the creative light
Of Earth's green hill.

seven

THE OLD HOUSE

The next Monday after Clay went to work, Dixie and I sat in front of the television, munching teriyaki chicken wings and drinking tea. My old buddy, guilt, crept in. There were starving children in Africa, and I was eating more than my share. My heroine, Heather, who'd been totally neglected and forgotten during our I-65 trip, needed me. She was still in limbo, pregnant and running away. It was time to save her.

But first I had to get off the couch and exercise, do some benevolent something, and return writing to its rightful place in my schedule, but I was too tired after my trip and it was too hot outside to walk. Also, before releasing me from the hospital, my doctor had given me a prescription to lower my blood pressure and told me I had to start eating better: more fruits and veggies and less junk food. For my health's sake, I knew I could do it. I'd just have to psych myself up.

I closed my eyes and envisioned myself healthier, wearing smaller, fashionable clothes, my hair and make-up perfect. A new and improved me sat in a chair next to Oprah and held up my best-selling novel. I could see myself and Oprah both smiling. The book jacket, though, was kind of fuzzy, sort of a maroon color with gold lettering, and I couldn't quite make out its title.

It didn't matter, however, because Scott called and said both he and his wife, Rachel, were working overtime and asked if I could take Catherine Lee and Mark shopping to buy their school clothes and supplies. Of course, I would, and yes, I'd pick them up from school every day to make sure they got home safely and stay with them until he or Rachel got home.

As I was getting ready to take the kids to the mall one afternoon, the tenant at one of the townhouses my husband and I rented out called and said the air-conditioning wasn't working. Then Clay called and asked if I'd pick up his shirts from the laundry and go to the drug store. Suddenly, I longed for those long, boring, lethargic days when I was trying to write.

Who knew there were so many errands to run and how in the world did I have time to fit all this in while I was writing? At least I was no longer sitting on the couch, watching TV while eating. I was waiting for hours in empty townhouses for plumbers, electricians, and cable guys, taking Catherine Lee and Mark to the doctor, dentist, soccer practice, and karate, rushing forgotten lunch money to the school, or retrieving cell phones that had been taken up by teachers. The townhouses I resented, but errands with and for my grandchildren and spending time with them gave me new purpose and energy.

By mid-August, with Catherine Lee and Mark in school and the vacant townhouse rented, Heather and I spent more time together in the mornings, and in the evenings I worked on my memoir. All was well in my world, crowded as it had become, until I went on a diet.

A few days before Labor Day, as my doctor had suggested and I had yet to comply with, I decided simply to eat less, a lot less, and exercise more. Breakfast was easy, a boiled egg and orange juice. I took Dixie for a walk, and when we returned I immediately sat down at my computer, reread the last chapter I'd worked on, and waited for the inspired words to course through my brain. Heather was nowhere to be found.

Good grief. Did I write that? No good. How could I have thought that was good? Rapidly I changed verbs, nouns, entire sentences, and paragraphs, and, in a few hours, had one page finished. Then I reread it. No, that wasn't right either. Why did I ever think I could write? My grandchildren could've written it better. I should never have quit work.

Well, it wasn't really that bad, was it? My stomach growled. I couldn't concentrate. All I could think about was bacon and eggs. But I couldn't give in. Could not eat. Not yet.

And I couldn't sit on the back porch or I'd spend all morning out there, and by noon the heat and inactivity would make me more tired than when I went to bed last night. Still no words would leap into my brain and out my fingers into the pen and onto paper. I couldn't sit in front of the TV and eat, so I did jumping jacks while watching the early news.

At about 10:00 my stomach was rumbling and moaning and felt kind of queasy; I felt faint and broke out into a cold sweat. Holding onto the refrigerator door, I searched its contents for relief. I'd eaten so appropriately for breakfast; I couldn't give up. What if I found the cure for overeating and wrote an award-winning book about it? I saw myself talking to Oprah AND Dr. Phil this time.

I ate an apple. The closet, that's what I'd do—finish cleaning the closet and then read F. Scott Fitzgerald for inspiration. Something was bound to come to me. I ambled to the overstuffed, now totally rearranged but still disorganized closet, gazed into it, and made a mental note of where things should go. Slowly, I moved a box from one side to the other. It was hard work and made me tired. *Little House on the Prairie* called me.

The apple didn't work. I was still hungry. At 10:30 I ate lunch, a leftover, dry, baked chicken breast and half of a cup of green beans. Ahh, much better. I felt completely full and satisfied—until about 11:00 a.m. Time for another boiled egg and grape juice. Still hungry. I watched the news and a commercial for Hardee's, but I didn't give in.

At 11:30 I rummaged through the refrigerator and found the remnants of a head of lettuce, a limp carrot, half an onion, and some shredded taco cheese. I took the green specks out of the cheese, threw everything into a bowl, and started to eat. It was terrible until I put a smidgen of ranch dressing on it. Not great but almost edible. A tiny bit more of the dressing and it might be good enough to eat. Then another tablespoon. And another.

1:00 p.m. Ravenous. I had trouble concentrating on my soap opera, so I jumped up, found some cleanser, and frantically scrubbed the bathroom. The sink was kind of streaked, but I couldn't concentrate on it. I moved the box in the closet from its most recent position back to the other side. I gathered every towel, sock, and stray piece of clothing I could find and threw it into the washer. Raced back to the kitchen. No, I couldn't.

I did. I jerked a cheesecake from the freezer and ate it—the whole thing—still frozen. Between my soap and Dr. Phil, I drove to the nearest fast food place, bought a bucket of fried chicken, and ate it during Dr. Phil and a good portion of Oprah.

If I hadn't had to pick up Catherine Lee and Mark, I might've eaten the leftover pizza from three nights ago and the almost full half-gallon of chocolate chip ice cream.

When Clay came home that night, he looked at me and at the mountain of dishes in the sink and said, "What'd…"

I squinted my eyes and dared him to finish the sentence.

He didn't.

"You know what I need?" I called out to Clay, who'd poured himself a drink and was settled in front of the evening news. "A family reunion. Like the ones Mother's family had when I was little." I didn't know where that idea came from, but when the words popped out of my mouth, it started rolling around in my mind and wouldn't let go.

"Uh-huh." No movement from him.

"Next June. At the cemetery in Nectar. Where my grandparents are buried. Where we used to go to all-day-singings and dinner on the ground."

No answer.

"Don't know why they called it that. There were actually long tables covered with fried chicken, pies, cakes, potato salad. Best food I ever had anywhere."

Clay said nothing. Some TV anchor talked about the war in Iraq.

"I think it was on Mother's Day every year, and we decorated the graves and all the women wore carnation corsages. Those whose mothers were still alive wore red and those whose mothers had died wore white. It wasn't sad, though. Are you listening to me?"

"Uh-huh," he lied. He had no idea what I was talking about. And didn't care.

I said something I shouldn't have and stalked off to the back porch to sulk. A redbird landed on one of the rose bushes and stared at me. Maybe it felt protected by the screen and distance that separated us or maybe it was just a bold bird, but it held that stare for a long time. I stood up and moved toward it. It didn't move.

I wiped sweat from my forehead, opened the door, and walked out into the late-afternoon sunshine. The redbird still stared. I sat in a lawn chair, my skin and clothes moist, my face burning, and tried to communicate with it by thinking bird thoughts. The first thing that came into my mind was, "Are you crazy? Out here in the heat when you could be in the shade of your porch under a ceiling fan?"

The second thought that sprang into my mind was, "Yes." I went back inside and turned toward the bird. He was gone. But he left me with a new insight: I wasn't crazy; I missed my original family, especially Mother and Brother who'd loved me unconditionally and cared about practically everything I said, did, or felt. Never again would I be their adored little girl, showered with attention. I'd never sit safely and securely in Mother's lap enveloped in the aroma of her Chanel No. 5, feel the gentle touch of her hand on my forehead when I was sick, see my brother's crooked smile, or hear his easy laugh.

No, there'd be no reunion. Most of the people I'd known and loved as a child were gone. But I could write about them in the memoir I'd started, let them live again on paper, in my heart, and, perhaps, in the hearts of my children and grandchildren. I retrieved my notebook, sat at the table on the back porch, and started writing.

What happened next was very strange, as if my cousin Jenny received some kind of psychic message from me. After several years of not communicating with each other, that evening, while I was still longing for and writing about my childhood family, she called. We talked about our shared memories and vowed to email and talk to each other more often. Which we did.

Later that night, I searched through old boxes and files until I found "The Earthquake," the story I'd written in 1992 after my stepfather died and I had to go into the empty house I'd shared for most of my childhood with him, Mother, and Brother.

THE EARTHQUAKE

With its porches and wings jutting out in all directions and its yellow aluminum siding gleaming in the sunshine, the house smiled warmly and invited me in. So, why did I hesitate? My footsteps struck the rock walkway, scattering dried, dead leaves and crunching them beneath the soles of my Nikes. My heart pounded and my stomach churned as I took slow, tentative steps toward the house. The rest of the world seemed to stand still. No breeze, no birds, no children riding their bicycles. No cars zooming down the street. Just me and the house on that cold January day. And I could have sworn I heard it whisper my name, begging me to save it.

We had grown up together, that house and me. When Mother and my stepfather first bought it, there were only six small rooms and a bath, but after numerous remodeling jobs that stretched out over forty years, it had plumped and fattened to ten rooms, a garage, several storage areas, and two bathrooms. They also installed a screened-in porch complete with refrigerator, table, and chairs—a great place to sip coffee early in the morning or eat watermelon and barbecue on the Fourth of July.

Sitting in Mother's favorite lounge chair on the front porch, I reached into my purse and pulled out the latest obituary. But tears clouded my vision and I couldn't see the words I'd memorized or the fuzzy newsprint picture of my stepfather, so I carefully folded it and slipped it inside the plastic pocket in my wallet. In a few days, when I could bring myself to open the cedar chest, I would place it in there with my mother's and brother's obituaries.

They were gone forever, all the people who had been with me since my birth, who had comforted or celebrated with me when my dog died, my boyfriend dated my best friend, I married, my children were born, when I divorced, and through all the ups and downs that create a life. And now even the old house that had sheltered us through it all would be gone, taken over and demolished by the city in the name of progress. How could I possibly go through its contents and disperse the memories of a lifetime? It lived and breathed and spoke to me.

Slowly, almost fearfully, I went inside. Every wall and floor, every picture and curtain, every crack and stain that were once so familiar, now seemed eerily strange. Except for the creaking of the floor when I walked, the house was still and quiet, and there was a peculiar lack of odor.

I slid my hand across the cool glass of the oak curio cabinet left by my grandmother and through the dust that had never been allowed to gather on the coffee table. In the center of the table was a flowerpot in the shape of a gray elephant wearing a crimson shirt with bright white letters that read "Alabama." It looked out of place there, but because I had given it to her, Mother had proudly displayed it.

Gathering some of her photo albums from their perch on the top of the long unused Hi-Fi, I went into my bedroom and sat pensively on the same bed I'd slept in as a child.

Yes, I did smell something: Chanel No. 5, Mother's favorite perfume. Again, I was a teenager dressing for a date and Mother and I were going through our Saturday night ritual. Though she knew I didn't like to wear jewelry or perfume, right before it was time for me to leave, she adorned me with necklace, bracelet, and earrings, sprayed me with perfume, and stepped back and smiled. "Yes, that's better." I coughed, sputtered, and complained when she did this, but she always did it anyway, and I always wore them. I still do. She wanted me to get my ears pierced, but I was one for avoiding even the slightest pain at all costs, so I refused—until one day in the mall when we stopped at a jewelry counter.

"Why don't you sit right here and look at the watches?" she said. "I might buy one."

And before I knew it some woman came at me with what looked like a dentist's instrument, put holes in my earlobes, and sealed them with two tiny gold earrings. It was over before I could protest.

I lay on the bed; Mother sat beside me, talking to me as she had during our disagreements, quietly at first and then more vociferously. The more I argued, the louder she got. Funny, those arguments seemed so important to me then, but now I can't remember what they were about.

From the kitchen the aroma of her marvelous pot roast enticed me. The teenaged me wandered in and lifted the top of the electric skillet. For a few minutes I watched the meat, covered with potatoes, carrots, and onions, bubbling in its juices, and opened the oven door so the aroma of the cornbread mixed with that of the pot roast. At the sink, while drying pots and pans, Mother sang "How Great Thou Art," off-key of course, making up her own lyrics when she forgot the real ones.

"If I clean up as I go," she said, "I don't have so much to do after dinner."

Though not a great chef, she loved to cook for us and we loved to eat her food. After my brother and I were grown, she always sent us home with "care packages" of leftovers. How I longed to hug her one more time and tell her how much those dinners and care packages meant to me.

The unmistakable aroma of Old Spice filtered into the kitchen as a plastic spider jumped into the sink. Mother and I winked at each other and squealed, more to delight Chick, my stepfather, who was standing in the hallway laughing, than out of any real fright.

I saw the four of us—Mother, Chick, Brother, and me—as we came back from one of our shopping trips. We were the only family I knew who made grocery shopping a pleasurable excursion. Suddenly, Chick threw a jar of mayonnaise to Brother, who was standing beside the pantry. "Catch!" he called out. Brother, surprised yet not surprised, never missed.

Who but my stepfather could make a mundane drive to the country fun? With a funny, crooked smile, he'd say, "Let's just turn down this road and see where it takes us." A few minutes later, still smiling, he'd say, "Wow, we must be lost." And Brother and I would excitedly tell him which turns to take until we were finally "found." Many times in later years I'd asked, "Were we really lost?" He never told me. I wished to be able to hug him one more time and tell him how much his dry wit and sense of humor meant to me.

Brother whistled as he set cans, jars, and bottles on the shelves. As usual, the tune was both familiar and unrecognizable. Laughing, he chased me through the house with a water gun and I shrieked as the water trickled down my back and my wet blouse clung to my skin. We ran through the house and out the front door; it slammed with a bang. Moments later, we came back in, arguing.

"I said do the dishes!" he shouted.

"No, you're not my mother."

"But I'm in charge." He hit me on the shoulder.

No pain, but I still managed to conjure up a good cry. "I'm telling on you. Just wait till Mother gets home."

"That didn't hurt." No sympathy from him.

"It did too."

"Did not."

"Did too." Louder crying. More sobs.

"Look," Brother said as he picked up an empty Coke bottle, "if that hurt, you can hit me with this."

Silence. Was he kidding? That'd never happened before. I took the empty bottle and hit him across the ear with all the strength I could muster. He looked stunned, and I was immediately sorry I did it. I don't remember who did the dishes, but I do remember that my brother never again gave me any weapons to use against him.

Outside, towering George ambled down the street. He was at least in the sixth grade, bigger than most of the other kids on the block, and for some reason liked to pick on me.

"Gimme that rope," he demanded.

I kept on jumping.

"Gimme the rope!" he screamed.

I kept on jumping. Suddenly, he reached out and grabbed it as it swung over my head.

"I told you to gimme the rope."

What else to do but cry. "I'm telling Brother on you," I sobbed.

He looked around. No brother in sight. "So what? Go ahead and tell 'im. I ain't afraid of 'im." He made some awkward attempts to jump the rope while making fun of me.

I ran toward Suzanne's house, still crying and screaming. Sure enough, he was there. For reasons unknown to me, my brother and his friends thought that if they climbed the trees in front of her house that she would notice them. They even took turns lying in the street until a car came along—to see who would lie there the longest before he jumped up and got out of the way. I don't recall a car getting anywhere near close, and I know for a fact that Suzanne thought they were a little strange, but I never told them. It was too much fun to watch.

Ever the protector, he called to his friends, "Be right back!" and walked with me toward home. "I'll take care of it," he comforted me. But by the time we got there, George was gone and the jump rope was lying on the sidewalk. He patted me on the back and I watched him walk away to join his friends. With each step, the sidewalk and street behind him cracked a little, growing longer and wider.

There had been an earthquake and my childhood was on the other side of the ravine.

Hugging Mother's photo albums close to me, I walked slowly downstairs, sat in the midst of boxes filled with memories, and turned the pages that contained and bits and pieces of my family's history.

They were all there: the people I loved as babies, children, teenagers, adults, and those who had grown old. They smiled, laughed, frowned, and made faces at the camera; they celebrated birthdays, vacations, graduations, weddings, and Christmases. There were old sepia prints of people I didn't know, and there were pictures of flowers taken at funerals.

It's been years since that day, and though it no longer stands on top of the hill, I occasionally drive up there and an ethereal old house with gleaming yellow aluminum siding appears on the vacant land. I watch two children playing, a brother and a sister, and I hear their mother calling them inside for dinner and their stepfather asking if they want to go for a ride in the country.

And sometimes when I least expect it, I become my mother, standing at the sink, washing dishes and singing, off-key of course, "How Great Thou Art," while the pot roast cooks.

eight

HUH? DID YOU HEAR THAT?

It was the coolest Labor Day I could remember in my sixty something years—overcast, occasional drizzles, the temperature hovering around 70 degrees. Yet there I was in the swimming pool in Darrin and Kelly's backyard, throwing the beach ball to Mark and Catherine Lee while contemplating Heather and how to describe the cold numbness of her body and the crackle of her footsteps as she ran across the frozen snow. I jumped, jogged, and twisted, trying to keep warm but wasn't able to stop the shivering. I was cold, numb, miserable, happy, and exhilarated.

We were all together—my husband, four children, and their families. Above the splashing and playing in the pool, I could hear them laughing and talking—the hum of brotherly and sisterly camaraderie. The moments a mom whose children grew up and left home dreams of, especially when said mom had for years told those kids that someday they'd be grown and would love and get along with each other.

I could almost see Darrin punch Cathy in the arm and hear him shout, "Mom, she tore up my Matchbox city!"

And little Cathy screaming because a roly-poly had crawled on her toe as she tried to dig up daffodils with one of my grandmother's sterling silver spoons.

"They won't hurt you," I said in my gentle, soothing, motherly tone.

It didn't help. She ran, shrieking, into the house.

I looked at Darrin and his friend who were also in that long-ago yard, with boards, wire, and string, setting a trap and trying not to giggle. I gave him my meanest stare. Not only for teasing his sister but because he liked to catch snakes.

Shrugging his shoulders, he confessed, "We might've told her roly-polies were poisonous and would make her sick and she'd die." He paused, snatched the string, watched the wire cage thing fall, then added, "We were just having fun. Didn't mean to scare her."

Nostalgic and misty-eyed, I climbed out of the pool, wrapped a towel around my shivering body, and sauntered over to join my children. Maybe reminisce a little.

As I got closer, however, I stopped in my tracks. There was something strange about my beloved family. They were huddled in a circle, every one of them bent toward the center, whispering, totally unaware that I was approaching.

I know I heard Cathy say, "Green beans."

And Diana said something about, "Hearing loss."

I sauntered over to them and asked innocently, "What's going on?"

They stopped talking abruptly, straightened their backs, and stared at me as if trying to come up with an explanation. I scrutinized their faces. Awkward silence.

Suddenly, Diana said, "Has anyone seen my football schedule? I'm sure I left it right there." She pointed to the picnic table with the huge green-striped umbrella over it. Towels, paper cups, and several half-empty bags of assorted chips were scattered on top of the table.

"Yes, I think I saw it," Cathy answered hurriedly as she hopped up and pretended to look for the non-existent schedule. At the same time, the rest of them started looking and talking and I couldn't understand any of it.

"I'm going to get dressed," I announced. "But remember, it was just an accident. It could've happened to anybody."

"It's okay, Mom," Cathy said. "You just need a hearing aid."

There was nothing wrong with my hearing. I loved my quiet and peaceful world. It was everyone else who became irritable, screamed at me a lot, and forgot how to speak correct English. Well, maybe I couldn't hear quite as well as I used to. One time I heard Scott tell his children to watch out for signs of danger when Nana was driving because "she couldn't hear worth a flip." Or was it another word? But "couldn't hear worth a ship" didn't make sense.

Maybe my children had a point. After all, I'd read that people who didn't hear well might be at greater risk for Alzheimer's. What if I got that and had to be put in a nursing home? Maybe I ought to hurry and finish my novel before I forgot who I was. Or they'd have to hire a babysitter for me, and I'd never be alone again. Never have those stretches of uninterrupted time to think and write. Or I'd forget what I was writing and every day have to start something else.

"I know," I said as I walked slowly across the wooden bridge from the pool to the house, feeling older than Methuselah. "I'm going to get dressed now."

Then Cathy told them about the green beans.

It had happened on a cold, sunshiny day the previous March. Carly and I were sitting on the couch watching Dora the Explorer while Cathy took a long bath. Just as Dora took a map out of her backpack, Cathy stuck her head out of the bathroom door and said, "I hink it's time tonchunk baaaas."

"Huh?" That backpack could sing and dance, and when it asked which of three items would help Dora and Boots cross the stream, Carly called out, "Boat!" Just like her mom, she was super intelligent, and she had personality.

When Carly was one and we were all gathered around the Christmas tree ready to open presents, she had danced around in the center of the room wearing wrapping paper and red and green bows and sang, "Let's party!"

"Dabees!" Cathy screamed from the bathroom.

This was my morning time with Carly. Just her and me. And I wanted to enjoy it before she grew up, but I answered, "What'd you say?"

"Dagrabends."

Suddenly, just as the fire alarm went off and smoke rolled in from the kitchen, my sweet daughter, wrapped in a towel and dribbling water all over my new hardwood floors, ran from the bathroom through the den and into the kitchen screaming words I never taught her. She jerked the errant pot from the stove and threw it into the sink. The alarm kept howling.

"Oh, I forgot to check on the green beans," I said as I gazed at my green vegetable of the day, lying limp and charred all over my shiny white sink. My new, stainless-steel pot was black and clutching a layer of blackened beans to its bottom. That burned smell would be hard to get rid of. "Why didn't you remind me?"

Cathy, her hair wet and sudsy, stared at me with that long-suffering "I'm about to explode" look of hers before she stomped off toward the back door, hollering, "Dosom widda arm!"

"Huh?" Alarm still screeching.

Speaking in words that in my day were reserved for sailors, she opened windows and the back door, and finally the noise subsided.

"Did you enjoy your bath?" I asked as politely as I could as I rejoined Carly in time for Dora and Boots to find the house across the stream and for Cathy to slam the bathroom door.

So I didn't hear as well as I used to. That didn't mean I had to wear hearing aids. After all, I'd tried them years ago and hated them. The first day I drove to work wearing my new in-the-ear devices, my car turned into a wind tunnel, fuzzing my thinking and drowning out the radio and whatever those angry people in the cars trying to pass me on the right were shouting. A couple of guys gave me the finger, and one dark-haired young woman who was talking on the phone and looking in the rear-view mirror while applying mascara almost hit me.

By the time I got to work, I'd bitten off two fingernails and was shaking with anxiety. I waited patiently for the elevator, and when the doors opened, I pushed the number six button and walked to the back. A bunch of people followed me. Second floor. More people. As usual, they all stood facing the front and not speaking. I was jammed into the back corner with an old man closing in on my personal space. The hearing aids picked that exact moment to squeal.

I turned my head to make them stop. It didn't help. The old man tried to step away from whatever was happening to me and bumped into the buxom blonde in front of him. She turned around.

"Watch it, George," she snapped.

He stepped backwards. I shook my head. But those hearing aids wouldn't quit singing, and now George and Blondie were arguing. Everyone in the elevator turned to look at me and got off when the doors opened on the fifth floor. Wonder what was going on in Engineering. Oh well, the darn things in my ear were silent by that time.

Until I got to my office. I thought it was a quiet, peaceful place to work. Boy, was I wrong.

The receptionist hollered, "Morning, Gayle!"

Pain struck my right ear. "You don't have to shout."

The copy machine was in the supply room next to the lobby, and I could hear it clicking, clicking, clicking. Was someone copying the national budget or *War and Peace*?

The coffee pot gurgled. Had it always been that loud? People laughed, complained, shuffled from one place to the other carrying their cups, and clunking them down on desks. Even the computers hummed incessantly, and the air conditioner noisily cranked out cold air.

On the verge of tears, I ran to the restroom to be alone and compose myself. Who knew pee hitting water could make so much noise? Or water hitting the sink? Or pulling paper towels from the holder that wouldn't let them go? *Help! Let me outta here!* I rushed down the hall and almost made it through the lobby.

"Are you okay?" my friend, Patty, asked as she put her arm around my shoulder.

More shrieking in my ears. Everyone stopped to gawk at me. I couldn't help it. I cried. So loud it made my hearing aids screech again. I ran to my office, yanked them from my ears, sat down at my desk, and returned to my quiet and peaceful world.

I figured someday I'd try the new digital ones. But right then I had to get back to my family, now clustered in the den and watching the Weather Channel to see how long the torrential rain and thunderstorm would last.

In my mind, however, was a new chapter about Heather and her family and their plot to help her against her will. The words and images flowed through my brain in a sequence as beautiful as the poetic prose written by F. Scott Fitzgerald. But when I finally found a pen and paper in a drawer in the kitchen, all those remarkable scenes had vanished.

The wonderful, boisterous sounds of laughter and chatter from the den had wiped out every negative thought and lured me into their weather-watching world.

nine

MY HEROINE, MY REDBIRD, AND KFC

By late October, Heather was embroiled in conflict with her husband, mother, and father. I'd completed four chapters, and she still didn't know which way to go or who to turn to. As I sat on the back porch pondering the different directions her life could take and her reactions to each, I admired the tenacious red roses that still clung to their bush despite the cooler weather and shorter days. The trees and other bushes around the roses had already turned red, brown, and gold and had dropped many of their leaves into a shaggy autumn carpet that covered much of the backyard.

A redbird landed on the rose bush and looked straight at me. At first, I wondered if the thorns didn't hurt his tiny bird feet, but then my mind moved on to messages. This little critter that still hung around in my yard after the others had left probably had a message for me that I needed to figure out. I kept going back to wondering why the thorns didn't hurt his feet. The bone spur on my left heel was causing me plenty of pain.

Yes, that was it. My next chapter would be about pain and suffering, and I'd start with the creeping onset of small but escalating physical pain that comes with old, uh, "mature" age. Of course, Heather was much younger than me; well, she was me when I was younger, but I had been her age when my feet had first started to hurt. Even though aching feet really aren't that interesting, they'd give her something else to contend with and fret about. Maybe I could have her walk to the Kentucky Fried Chicken in a snowstorm, with the white stuff already four feet deep. After all, I'd actually done that. I knew the frustration that drives mothers to do things they ordinarily wouldn't do.

It was a cold blustery winter when my four children were, well, children, and we lived outside of Chicago. It snowed. A lot. We had a white Halloween, followed by a white Thanksgiving, Christmas, and every day in between and thereafter.

Before my little darlings were scheduled to return to school from their Christmas vacation, it snowed some more. The heat went out in the school building and the children couldn't go back to school. When they could've gone back, the janitors went on strike. The darlings were home six weeks. In the middle of winter. With snow up over the shrubbery and wind chills below zero. I didn't work. I prayed for a job. I prayed for sanity. I prayed for world peace and, God, please let it start at my house.

One morning in about the fifth week of my confinement, the said angelic kids sat at the kitchen table, whining and fussing about their lack of an appropriate breakfast.

"Mom, you know I don't like frosted flakes."

"Mom, I want the rest of the pizza for breakfast."

"Mom, he got the prize yesterday. It's my turn."

In my most loving, motherly way, I told them to shut up.

"Mom, she's looking at me."

"I want a peanut butter sandwich."

"I'm not hungry."

"She's still looking at me."

Two of them, I don't remember which two, tugged at the cereal box until they both let go and tiny flakes of corn exploded all over the table and floor. I wanted to beat them all and choke them with my bare hands, but I loved them, so I bit my arm. It bled. I cried.

"What's the matter with you?" Darrin asked.

It was too much for a mother to bear. Every nerve in my body jangled. My insides shook. I threw a banana at my son. When he dodged, it hit the window, which cracked but didn't shatter. Darrin's face registered the same surprised non-belief my husband's had the day I ran over something in the road that bounced up and hit the underside of the car and caused some yucky, slick substance to leak onto the garage floor.

All four of my children stared at me. No one moved or said anything. For the first time in their young lives, they were afraid of me. I was conflicted. Should I say nothing to soothe them and enjoy the blissful silence? Maybe I should hug Darrin and tell him I was sorry I'd thrown a banana at him and that I'd never do it again. I wondered if I'd scarred him for life. Would he and the other children ever get over having a mother who threw bananas at them?

No need for guilt. After a couple of minutes of blessed silence, all of my children began arguing in unison about whose fault it was that I was in such a bad mood. Still quarreling, they all galloped into the den to destroy it too.

For lunch I wanted Kentucky Fried Chicken. I had to have it. With lots of grease and crust. However, driving was impossible. The streets in our neighborhood hadn't been salted or plowed. That once beautiful, waist-deep, white stuff now covered the yard, sidewalks, and street, and frozen, gray and black slush adorned the gutters. On both sides of our driveway were snow banks at least eight feet high where my two older children had shoveled it every day for weeks.

But I was determined. I put on my undershirt, shirt, sweater, stockings, socks, long underwear, pants, coat, gloves, earmuffs, hat, scarf, and fur-lined boots. I left my older daughter, then about fourteen, in charge and told the kids they'd better mind her and behave while I was gone.

It was two miles to the KFC, and with every step I had to lift my leg up out of the snow and put it back down. Up, down, up, down. Wind and a jillion tiny pellets of snow stung my eyes and nose. Cold penetrated my face and somehow through my boots to my poor aching toes.

All the way, struggling to stay upright and pushing against the wind, I prayed for poor Diana at home with her three younger siblings. Please, God, let me move home to Birmingham where it rarely snows and two inches is a holiday. I promised if He did, I'd never live in a cold-weather climate again (He did, and I haven't).

When I finally got to the chicken store, the woman behind the counter said, "Did you blow in from the North Pole?"

I didn't smile. I didn't smile again until I opened the door to my house and found Diana and Darrin quietly playing The Game of Life at the dining room table. Cathy and Scott were taking naps.

There was a God, after all, and I thanked Him.

On my back porch that October day, my mind wandered from that long-ago frozen winter, to the redbird, to Heather. Like me, Heather wasn't fond of cold weather. What if she somehow got lost in the snow? And she was pregnant? What if her husband was trying to find her? My pen started moving and so did Heather. She, too, put on her overcoat, gloves, and hat, but forgot her boots, and headed out into the bitter cold night. As the snow seeped through her socks to her feet, pain stabbed her toes.

Two hours later, after I got Heather to the hospital, I put my pen down and looked up. The early afternoon sun had disappeared behind ominous gray and black clouds with a strong wind pushing them across the sky. Thunder rumbled in the distance. I looked for my redbird to thank him for his insight. He was nowhere to be found. I thanked him anyway, picked up pen and paper, and tried to stand up quickly so I could hurry inside to warmth and shelter. Uh oh. I'd spent too many hours sitting and had forgotten to get up and stretch every thirty minutes. My neck creaked, my back ached, and my legs were numb. I sort of moseyed in an upward direction.

At that exact minute, streaks of lightning lit up the sky, followed by a loud roar. I sprinted for the kitchen door. Okay, it may have been a stroll for some people, but for me, with my feet throbbing with every step, it was a run. Dixie passed me and didn't stop until she flopped, hyperventilating, on the floor of my closet. A minute or so later, also hyperventilating, I held onto a box, slid down beside her, took my shoes off, and stretched my legs out in front of me. Even the soft carpet against my left heel made it hurt.

The closet had no windows, so I couldn't see the outside world, but I could definitely hear it. And it sounded like the house might fall down around me. Okay, Gayle, calm down. It'll end soon. Don't panic. It's just a storm. Not as bad as seeing a copperhead coiled and ready to strike. Dixie curled into a ball behind a box. I pulled her into my lap, rubbed her back to comfort her and said in my soothing, baby-talk voice, "It's okay. We're going to be just fine."

It was the same way Mother used to comfort me during a storm. Suddenly, I missed her desperately and longed for some connection to her. With the noise of thunder, rain, and wind as melancholy background music, I searched through my notebooks until I found the one from the summer of 1990 and started reading. It was filled with words of despair and fear. My mother was dying from cancer. What would I do without her? She'd been there with me through every crisis of my life. But there was hope, wasn't there? A miracle? My words written so long ago were so dismal that I cried reading them that day in the closet.

When the storm abated, I returned to the back porch to work on my almost-forgotten memoir.

ten

THANKSGIVING, CHILDREN, IN-LAWS, AND KNIVES

After the doctor stuck a needle in my heel, an experience I hope never to have again, the pain from the bone spur subsided. I resumed my walks and quit screeching out in pain and saying stuff my mother would have spanked me for saying. By mid-November I'd finished my memoir and, with the help of my computer, had turned it into four books, which were wrapped and ready to be put under the Christmas tree. I was proud of this accomplishment and ready to get Heather out of the hospital. She'd been languishing around the emergency room too long and was getting impatient.

Then the holidays struck. I've read that lots of writers have trouble getting anything done this time of year. What with all the shopping, planning, parties, and eating. It certainly proved true for me. In addition to all that, I had a newly vacated townhouse to get cleaned up, painted, and rented, and of course I enjoyed picking up Catherine Lee and Mark from school each day.

But I had to find time for Heather. Anytime I paused, like waiting in line at the bank or at the checkout at Walmart, there she was, clamoring for attention. Late one night, wearing fuzzy, pink house shoes and a long dark-green robe, I sat on the back porch and gazed at the half-moon and stars against a navy-blue sky. Heather sat on the other side of the table.

"I've got to get out of this hospital," she said.

"I know. I'm trying."

She was wearing one of those ugly hospital gowns and fidgeted with the string at the back of her neck. "It won't stay tied," she said.

"Where do you want to go when you leave?" I asked. "Back to your husband? Maybe stay with your mom for a while?"

"I don't know."

"I'll figure it out."

"Soon?" she asked.

"As soon as the holidays are over."

The next day I sent email invitations to all my children for Thanksgiving dinner, realizing they all had commitments of their own—jobs, husbands or wives, as well as children. Three of them lived out of town. If they couldn't come I'd understand. Wouldn't be at all disappointed. Well, not much. The holidays were the only time of year I got to see my whole family, all of my children, daughters-in-law, sons-in-law, and grandchildren at the same time. They were the highlights of my life, and I was blessed to have a good relationship with each of them.

The first time I met Cathy's husband, Charles, I was a single mom and my mother, stepfather, and I were trying to get a huge Christmas tree through the door of my small townhouse. I looked up and spotted Cathy strolling hand-in-hand with Charles down the sidewalk toward us. What I actually saw was a strong, handsome young man with lots of gorgeous dark hair—one who could wield a chainsaw without injuring himself or us.

Before he was introduced, before anyone could say anything, I handed him the chainsaw and said, "The trunk's too big for the stand, and we can't get it through the front door."

"Yes ma'am," he said.

The chainsaw buzzed and twigs and branches flew across the sidewalk and yard. The tree lost a lot of its height and fullness, but he fixed the problem. We were instant friends.

A few months later, before Cathy and Charles were engaged or had even talked about it, they were having lunch with me, Diana, Darrin, and Scott. While the rest of them sat around the table, laughing and talking, Charles was helping me. At the time I wasn't sure if he felt sorry for me, darting around my own kitchen, trying to find lost ingredients and, when not found, hunting substitutes for them, or if he was trying to impress me. Anyway, that day, he was looking for a spice rack containing pepper, salt, and garlic. I didn't have one. I think he was going to ask me where the spices were kept, because he turned toward me and said, "Ga," then after a pause, "Mo." Another pause. Everyone stopped talking. They didn't move. All eyes were on Charles. What would he call me?

Trying to be helpful, quickly and without thinking, I said, "It's hard to figure out what to call your mother-in-law, isn't it?"

Everyone laughed, except Charles.

The first time I met Christopher, Diana had just run a marathon and was tired and weepy. He sat with her in my living room on Mother's pale green Victorian couch, the one she'd worked, scrimped, and saved for a year to be able to buy and wouldn't let anyone sit on, and tried to comfort my daughter. I knew then he was a keeper. He'd been helping me with various projects ever since. Every weekday he worked with computers, so I figured it was only natural that on his days off he should want to spend his time fixing ours, which he did without complaint almost every time he visited.

Darrin's wife, Kelly, was always quiet, kind, thoughtful, and polite, and we both loved my son. She, however, had something special for me. She worked in a doctor's office, and I always had questions. Like the time I stared into her eyes with my eyes opened as wide as I could get them and asked, "See all that red?"

"Yes." How could she miss it? I looked like I'd been on a three-week bender.

"Is it pink eye?" I asked.

"I don't think so. Probably allergies. You might want to try some over-the-counter drops. If that doesn't work, check with your doctor."

Though Scott and Rachel are now divorced, during that Thanksgiving she was still an integral and much-loved part of our family. She was the efficient, energetic one who could finish the task while I was still thinking about it. Whether we were at their house or at ours, she always had dinner prepared and on the table while I searched for the onions or catsup, and after dinner she had the dishes in the dishwasher, food put away, table wiped down, and floor swept while I searched for a container for the left-over potatoes.

All my children said they'd be here for Thanksgiving. In anticipation of having my family together, I started concentrating on cooking the perfect turkey dinner, something that didn't come natural to me.

One time when Scott was about six, he said, "I'll be glad when you grow up to be a grandmother and learn to cook." Another time, he asked, "Why is it when

Mawmaw's at our house she does all the cooking and when we're at her house she does all the cooking?"

I sat on Mother's couch and gazed at the portrait of her hanging above her antique china cabinet. "Where'd I go wrong, Mother?" I asked. She'd always been able to put together a perfect holiday, complete with turkey, dressing, ham, sweet potatoes, a home-made carrot cake with real carrots, date cookies, and all the scented memories of my childhood.

My kids have memories of countless trips to the grocery store to get things I'd forgotten, of meatloaf so greasy the dog wouldn't eat it, the strawberry pie we had to drink, the dressing as dry as sand and with the taste of a bowl of wet flour, and my ten-alarm chili they'd washed down with gallons of iced tea.

My children told me it was ADD, and I have to admit that organization and focus are a bit of a problem for me, especially when it concerns menus and cooking. After considerable thought and contemplation, I swore Clay to secrecy and hired a friend, who had owned a restaurant and was a great cook, to prepare and deliver dinner before my family arrived.

During Thanksgiving dinner, Cathy smiled and said, "Wow, Mom, this is the best Thanksgiving dinner you ever made."

Diana, Darrin, and Scott also raved about the sweet potato casserole, dressing, and the wonderfully moist turkey. It went on for several minutes. They knew. They all knew. At least, they thought they knew. I didn't admit anything and neither did Clay.

"What time is the big game Saturday?" I asked, trying to change the subject. Diana went to Alabama; Cathy went to Auburn. Almost all of them loved to talk football.

Ahhh. Great food. Fun conversation. I'd done it. The great Thanksgiving deception—until Charles, Cathy's husband, who has a wicked sense of humor, said, "Did you mean to leave that big, empty box from Meemaw's Country Cooking in the garage?"

Busted. "No," I answered, smiling.

"Are you going to tell us what was in the box?" Charles asked.

"No," I said. No elaboration needed. I did, however, resolve to cook the best Christmas dinner anyone ever put on a table.

A couple of weeks before Christmas, I decided to practice cooking something that didn't come in a can or frozen in a box, something that had to be put together and cooked on the stove. I settled for a roast. How difficult could it be? I had the meat in a baking pan with potatoes and carrots around it and was happily cutting onions and celery when Clay came home from work.

"What're you doing?" he asked before he even threw his car keys on the counter.

"Cooking."

The keys jangled as they hit the Formica. "But you're using a butcher knife," he said. "Here, let me help you." He took the knife from my hand and threw it into the sink but didn't finish the onions or celery. Would my family never forget the frozen turkey incident?

I wasn't sure whether to be grateful or angry. "I can still use my hands," I said.

"At least the onions weren't frozen," he said as he sailed into the bedroom to change clothes.

I put the lid on the roast, stuck it in the oven, and marched to the back porch, leaving the partially-sliced vegetables on the cutting board. The temperature was hovering around sixty degrees, but it was sunny with high cumulous clouds decorating the sky. Dixie followed me. My redbird was nowhere in sight.

Maybe Clay was right. My hands ached, had trouble grasping small objects, like pens or earrings, and often dropped larger items, like knives or skillets. The problem, however, had started years before the turkey accident, probably caused by all those years of typing. After all, I'd learned to type on an old-fashioned manual typewriter, one with no plugs, no electrical anything to help.

Just my fingers pounding those round buttons and pushing that return carriage in perfect rhythm. Clack, clack, push, clack. Suddenly, boinnnnnggggg. Wrong key. And with three carbon copies, too. I'd get out the old eraser, pull back the pages. Erase, smudge. Erase, smudge. Jerk out the paper. Start over. When that liquid, white wipe-out stuff came along, I thought it was God's greatest gift to womankind—no, second greatest. Cary Grant was first.

I didn't even notice my fingers were damaged until the spring before I left my long-time job at the law office. It was a clear, sunny day that held the hope of summer and warmth. I was admiring myself in the bathroom mirror, the one with perfect lighting. That morning, however, I happened to look down at my hands. Great gasps of breath. It couldn't be. No way. Wrinkles on the backs of my hands. And a small hard knob of a thing on the joint of both forefingers. My ring finger curved to the right.

At work, later that morning, I picked up the stapler and dropped it on my right big toe. I tried to look up a word in my Webster's New Collegiate Dictionary, rarely used because of the computerized thesaurus. I felt sorry for it sitting up on that top shelf, dusty and alone. Of course, I dropped it. Same toe.

I might have yelled a few things inappropriate for a grandmother in a quiet, dignified law office. Three admins and two lawyers rushed into my office. From the reception area I heard one frantic feminine voice say, "911?"

That evening I couldn't get the jar of peanut butter open. My hands ached, my head throbbed. I'd had a bad day, and I needed my comfort food. A jar opener. Yes, there was one. Somewhere. Not in the silverware drawer. Not in the utensil drawer. Not in the refrigerator. I threw the peanut butter across the room just as my husband, the ultimate jar opener, appeared in the doorway and dodged a flying missile.

The doctor said I didn't need tranquilizers, but it would help my hands if I spent a lot less time hunched over a computer typing, which was nearly impossible in a busy law office. Pain is a powerful motivator, and I wanted my hands to quit hurting, so, I chose to leave the co-workers I loved like family and find something that required less typing.

My next job was at a church with a food pantry. We'd received a whole slew of huge frozen turkey breasts. Susan, the other lady who worked there, and I decided we could feed more people if we thawed them in the refrigerator enough to cut them in half.

She cut hers. No problem. I cut one. No problem. The second one. A problem. I could tell because blood dribbled down the knife, onto and around the frozen poultry, and puddled on the counter. Holding my right hand in my left, I walked, leaving a trail of red blobs in the hallway, sanctuary, and vestibule into Susan's office.

"Do you think I need to go to the doctor?"

She drove me to the hospital.

When I got home after my surgery, while Diana and Cathy were still there to help me, I decided I wanted a ham sandwich. With my left hand—my right arm was in a cast—I looked in the knife drawer. No knives. In the silverware drawer. No knives. I opened every drawer in the kitchen. There was nothing sharper than a teaspoon. Not even my favorite pair of scissors.

"How am I going to slice this ham?" I asked whoever might be listening.

No one was.

"I've got to have a ham sandwich," I called out.

Diana sailed sweetly into the kitchen, smiled her guess-what-I'm-the-mother-you're-the-daughter-now smile, and said, "I'll cut that for you, Mom."

"What?"

She took the ham tenderly from my hands. "I'll do it."

"In the hall?"

"You sit down. I'll cut the ham for you."

"What?" I didn't know what she said, but she was taking my ham from me, and she didn't even like ham. I grabbed it.

She yanked it back. "Give me the damn thing. I'll cut it for you."

"Where are the knives?" I demanded.

I heard what she said next, and it wasn't pretty. About that time my traitor husband appeared with my favorite knife and handed it to Diana. She cut the ham, made my sandwich the way I like it, and brought it to me. Later, she cooked dinner and cleaned up the kitchen. When she eventually had to return to work, Clay, who is a worse cook than me, got take-out for us, and those wonderful, thoughtful church ladies brought us dinner for weeks.

I was beginning to enjoy the attention and sitting on the back porch talking to my redbird, writing for long stretches of time, and watching TV. As the weeks wore on, I spent more time watching TV than writing. Clay got tired of fast food and leftovers, and the church ladies' visits were less and less frequent. That's when the southern-woman's guilt complex set in. My hand was better, but I liked doing nothing. After all, I was still tired and occasionally there was a throb in my hand. For six weeks I reigned queen of my tiny world, but one day it abruptly ended. The doctor took the cast off, pronounced me well, and sent me to physical therapy. I had to go back to work and begin doing my share of the housework again.

After a while, almost everyone forgot about the accident and treated me normally—except Clay and my daughters. I felt normal, but my family obviously didn't think I was. They talked to me as if I were a toddler. "Here, let me do that for you," or, "I don't know where the knives are." I wanted to scream, "I can cut my own banana and spread my own peanut butter! Where are the knives?" It was a conspiracy.

Looking back, I realize I learned a couple of things that are still with me today. First of all, never cut anything frozen, especially a turkey. I still refuse to buy a frozen Thanksgiving or Christmas turkey; I wait until the day before the event and buy a fresh one. Sometimes I get one of those frozen-to-oven ones and never tell my family. They don't know the difference.

The second thing is that too much pampering is addictive. After my surgery, when every tiny movement of my hand triggered pain, I appreciated my children and Clay bringing me stuff and asking if I was okay and friends bringing us dinner every night. The thing was, after that part ended, I missed the attention. Those days of recovery reminded me of my childhood and my mother taking care of me when I was sick. If I closed my eyes I could feel her hand touch my forehead. I could smell the camphorated oil as she gently stroked it onto my chest and hear her soothing voice tell me, "You're going to be fine" and "I love you."

The one thing my family has never quit doing: hiding the knives. I keep telling them I've learned my lesson and that I can cut into a stick of butter without slicing into my fingers. If I want a slice of roast beef or tomato for my sandwich, I do it when I'm alone or sure they're not looking. To this day, if they catch me using a sharp knife, they say, "Here, I'll do that," and take it from me. I've learned to just let them. After all, they don't know that I found a rusty old butcher knife that had once belonged to my grandmother in my memory box. I hid it between the mattress and box spring. Just in case.

eleven

THE WEEK BEFORE CHRISTMAS
AND ALL THROUGH MY LISTS

A week before Christmas, I sent out an email asking all of my children what they wanted to bring for Christmas dinner. After I received their answers and shared them with Cathy, who has a great need to plan ahead, know everything that might happen, and act accordingly, she revised her detailed list of everything I'd need to buy.

I rearranged her list according to the layout of the store—fruits and veggies at the top because it was the first section on the right of the store, bakery stuff next, and so on. I spent hours cutting out coupons and arranging them in order.

When I got to the store, however, I opened my purse to pull out my list. No list. No coupons. I went back to the car and searched. No list. I had a decision to make, go home and try to find it or try to remember what was on it. I chose the latter.

Okay, first, produce. Got that. On to bakery. Got that. Coffee and creamer. I was doing so well. Oh, yes, I forgot the bananas. Back to produce. And I needed milk. On the back wall. And peanut butter, Aisle 4.

I stopped, took a deep breath and tried to think. Wouldn't date cookies be good? Where in the world would I find them? As I was looking, I passed canned vegetables, so I picked up some green beans. That reminded me I needed frozen corn. Oh yes, and cereal. Aisle 3. And sage. Aisle 14.

When I finally got home, I was exhausted but thought I'd gotten everything I needed. I couldn't check it out, though, because I never did find Cathy's list. Or the coupons.

On Christmas day, the turkey was in the oven, and I was crumbling cornbread. The guys were in the living room noisily watching a football game; Catherine Lee and Mark were chasing Carly and Dixie through the house, and Cathy, Diana, and I were in the kitchen. Laughing. Talking. Catching up. On the radio Gene Autry sang *Rudolph, the Red-Nosed Reindeer* for the eleven hundredth time. Everyone was happy, having a good time.

And, honestly, I was happy, too. Just a bit jangled, with the noise and all. I stared at the cornbread, trying to figure out what went in next. Oh, yes, onions.

I'd bought already chopped up ones because I still wasn't allowed to use knives. Or at least I meant to buy them. I searched the refrigerator. No onions. I looked in the pantry. Where were they? I tried to visualize myself in the produce section. I remembered reaching for celery. Apples. Surely, I didn't pass by onions.

"They were on the list," Cathy said.

"List?"

"You remember. The list."

I love my sons-in-law and my daughters-in-law. They really are my family and seem to understand me as well as my own kids. Charles sauntered into the kitchen in time to hear me lamenting the lack of onions. He smiled at me and said, "I'll take this one."

"Okay, Mom, think. Do you need anything else?" Cathy asked. Poor Cathy. She was always trying to get me to think logically and make lists to help me get through life with less stress. Just like my brother did when I was young and starting out in life. I should've listened to him.

But I couldn't think. For some reason a lot of background noise stops my brain function. While I was still pondering what to do next, Catherine Lee and Mark rummaged through the refrigerator to find something to eat, even though the counter was full of stuff--a veggie tray, a fruit tray, chips, cookies. What else could they possibly want to snack on while they waited for dinner?

"Where's the ranch dip?"

"Dip?" I started to help them search when I noticed the sage on the top shelf and wondered how it got there, took it and started mixing it into the dressing.

That's when Darrin and Kelly walked innocently into the kitchen and without my usual polite hello, how are you and hug, I blurted out, "You know, Kelly, I've had this headache for about a week."

Mark had given up his search for food and found solace by torturing Carly. He picked her up, pretended to drop her, caught her and swung her around while she squealed and begged for more. Catherine Lee stopped in front of the fruit bowl, grabbed an apple slice, stuck it in caramel sauce and popped it into her mouth. When Carly tried to do the same, Mark pulled her back from the counter. She lunged. He pulled. Again. And again. Carly yelped like a wounded puppy, which prompted Dixie to bark and a chorus of disparaging male voices from the living room to shout some really bad stuff about the referee.

"Do you have sinus pressure?" Kelly asked.

I bent over to see if the area behind my nose and between my eyes felt heavier. "I think so."

"You should try a sinus rinse and if that doesn't work, some Sudafed." She looked pleadingly at Darrin and added, "Could we take this grocery store run?"

For a few minutes I stood in the kitchen, hands on hips, listening to the music and bedlam, and trying to think what to do next. More shouts of joy and dismay came from the living room, and the volume of the ballgame increased. A toy mouse sailed by my shoulder and landed on the floor near my foot, followed by Dixie, who galloped through, snatched it in her teeth, and dashed toward Mark, who called out, loudly, "Get it, girl. Drop, Dixie, drop, drop, Dixie, drop. DIXIE, I said drop."

I looked around, trying to think. Mashed potatoes. That's what we needed. I pulled a box of instant ones from the cabinet, but as I retrieved the milk from the refrigerator, the container slipped through my fingers. Milk spilled and splattered all over the sink, counter, and stove and dribbled onto the floor. It wasn't my fault. It was my poor aching hands. But I had to have milk to make the instant mashed potatoes.

During a commercial, Christopher came in, hugged me, and asked if I needed him to go to the grocery store. "Well, I do need some milk," I said. "And, if you don't mind, could you look at my computer when you get a chance? It's really, really slow."

"Of course," he said.

Diana moved boxes and cans around in the pantry. "Where's the tea? We should've already made it."

"I was going to get Milo's tea. Already made."

"Going to?"

"I was getting the butter when I remembered the tea, but on the way, I saw some bite-size brownies and thought they'd be good, so I picked them up, and I think I went back to, no, I was on the way back to get the tea when…" I stopped. I had forgotten what I was talking about. No one was listening anyway.

Christopher and Diana made the third grocery store run.

Dinner was almost ready. The dressing, green beans, mashed and sweet potatoes? All done. Cranberry sauce and gravy were out. Veggie and fruit trays out. Last but not least.

"I'll put the rolls in," Diana said as she searched through mountains of empty cartons and sacks.

"Rolls?"

During half-time, Darrin, Scott, Charles, and Christopher made the final grocery store run.

While I warmed the green beans and mashed potatoes, Cathy pulled out her notebook, surveyed the food, made notes, went through the cabinets and refrigerator, and made lists of what we still needed. "Whose turn is it?" she asked.

No one answered.

I slipped my oven mitts over my hands and lifted the 16 lb. turkey out of the oven. It was nowhere near done. But it should've been. It'd been in there longer than the directions indicated. An hour later, I repeated the process. Still not done. We began munching on chips and dip, sliced apples dipped in caramel sauce, and carrot sticks. Another hour. Almost. All of my wonderful, beautiful, intelligent, practically-perfect-in-every-way children and grandchildren were getting testy and refused to wait any longer. They started eating the sweet potato casserole, coconut pie and chocolate cake and, instead of being scattered throughout the house, they hovered over me and the oven. Finally, when I had stretched my last nerve to its limit, that stubborn bird was done, and we all ate again, thankfully and peacefully, already laughing about our late bird and entrenching that holiday into our collective funny memories to talk about at all succeeding Christmases.

As my children and grandchildren walked through the buffet line and arranged themselves in small groups in the dining room and kitchen, the background Christmas carols blended with the hum of their voices and laughter. On the tree, my children's and grandchildren's fuzzy cotton and paper ornaments hung proudly beside my mother's homemade, delicate egg-shell ones, and all were surrounded by multi-colored lights. Mingled with the scents of my childhood—sage, cinnamon, sweet potato casserole, coffee, peppermint—the scene took my thoughts on a trip back through time. Again, Mother laughed; my stepfather sang out "Ho, ho, ho," and my brother whistled "Jingle Bells." Warmth and love for my home and family, past and present, filled my mind and spirit as tears of gratitude and joy moistened my eyes.

That warm, fuzzy feeling lasted at least three minutes.

As if on cue, my today and ethereal yesterday families started heading for the kitchen, loitering around the dessert area or throwing their paper plates in the trash. Mother turned to my stepfather and said, "I can't believe she didn't use my good china."

After we had cluttered the kitchen beyond hope of ever recognizing it again, it was time for the presents. Adults and children moved exuberantly to the living room as if we were all five-years-old and waiting for Santa. I made a big production of getting my four original children to sit together on the couch and, before any other gifts were exchanged, handed them the identically-wrapped presents. Inside were the books. Well, not really books—they were actually white binders. I had personalized each cover with their names and with pictures of things that reminded me of them, such as apples for my school teacher and cameras for my photographer. Of course, I had to insert family histories, some of my short stories and poems, and the funny stories we all remember and refer to when we're together.

There were also pictures of their great-grandparents and stories I remembered about them. How my grandfather, when I was eight and he was dying of cancer, had let me crawl on him like a mountain and put pin curls in his hair, "fix" it, brush it out, and do it again. And how Mama Lap, my grandmother, used to cook in an old-fashioned pressure cooker and often would come running from the kitchen, shooing my cousin and me out the front door, shouting "It's gonna blow! It's gonna blow!" While I was writing their histories, I'd felt like a spiritual conduit between the late nineteenth century when they were born and the twenty-first century, when my youngest grandchild was born. Hopefully I was giving life and feelings and stories to those whose genetics we share, who are a part of us and who were real people—not abstract figures.

Their reactions were better than I had hoped. My four grown-up children behaved as if they were kids again, with surprise, laughter, and inquisitiveness. They flipped through pages, smiling, laughing, talking to each other. "Yes, I remember that." "Look at this one, you look like a scarecrow." After the initial excited phase, they settled into quiet contemplation—just before my oldest grandchild jumped from her place on the floor and started handing out the rest of the presents.

As a group, we are neither neat nor quiet. The buzz of voices drowned out Bing Crosby and his "White Christmas" and red, green, and gold paper and bows decorated my tables and floor.

A wisp of air touched my hand and Mother said, "Remember now?" I nodded, and she continued, "It was never about the food or presents or decorations. It was always about love and being together and the satisfaction of doing something for those you love most and having them all together for a few hours without the worries of life interfering."

I always knew that, but sometimes in the chaos of Christmas we forget, and I'd fretted over a late turkey and trying to get everything right instead of focusing on the fuzzy warmth of a loving family. But as Mother always said, something good can come out of dark circumstances and mistakes. Even minor ones. Right after Christmas, I became the proud owner of a brand-new stove that had never had a turkey baking in its belly.

twelve

A NEW YEAR'S SURPRISE

The day after Christmas, I was grateful for my noisy, laugh-filled holiday, and that my children had appreciated their books. After all the presents were unwrapped, the four of them sat around the dining room table, pointing out funny pictures and laughing at our old stories. But the last of my grown-up children and my grandchildren had left that morning, and the house, suddenly, seemed so empty.

As I sat in the midst of the remnants of Christmas— scraps of wrapping paper, red, green and gold bows, the barren tree, the scent of pine and peppermint candy— my heart ached to go back in time.

In my mind, Diana was still nineteen and had come home from college for the holidays to find her mom sick. My stomach felt queasy, my head and throat hurt, and

I was tired and cranky. She had placed a cool cloth on my forehead, held my hand, and said, "Mom, you really should eat more vegetables and exercise more. You won't get sick so much."

I hate it when my own words come back to haunt me. When my children were little, I thought they had to eat beets, in my mind the perfect health food. But they had other ideas and not just about beets but all veggies, especially Cathy.

Whenever I cleaned up the kitchen, I found the dreaded beets, green beans, turnip greens, roast beef, almost everything except potatoes and corn, under the rim of her plate, under the fruit in the bowl, in the dog's bowl, in her pockets. Diana and Darrin were subtler. They pushed their food around on their plates, spread it out, and made it look as if they'd eaten more than they had.

One time when my three older children were visiting their grandmother, I had to call the electrician. He moved a living room chair to get to the plug. I was aghast. Humiliated. Half of a moldy peanut butter sandwich stared at me. I couldn't think of what to say. Apologize? He didn't move or say anything either. Finally, I got a paper towel, picked it up and threw it out.

"Kids," I said.

He looked around. No children in sight. Only four-month-old Scott, and he was asleep in his playpen.

Scott had a different problem. He preferred playing to eating.

"Scott, it's time for dinner."

"In a minute."

Later. "Scott, come on. We're eating."

"I'm almost done."

"With what?"

From his room, pounding, clinking, quiet.

"We're eating without you."

"Okay." He appeared with an old radio, in pieces, that he couldn't put back together.

Later, Darrin showed him how.

After a few hours of nostalgic melancholy and tears, I went to the computer and sent each of my children an email, telling them I was proud of them and loved them. I also mentioned that, despite their concerns, I could still hear well enough to function, and I could honestly use a knife without harm to myself or others.

Thankfully, the house didn't stay empty long. I spent the next day and the rest of the week with Catherine Lee and Mark, but I still had a hard time shaking the gloominess.

On New Year's Day, while Clay watched countless hours of football, I sat at the dining room table with pen and notebook, longing for warm weather, the back porch, and my friend the redbird to talk to. Heather called to me, begging me to get her out of the emergency room, but I pushed her to the back of my mind. Usually an optimist and the one who went around telling others to think positive, I battled one negative thought after another.

What if the clouds never went away and we never saw sunshine again? Everyone would be flying in the daytime, so they could get above the dark gloom. Night flights would vanish. What would happen to my grandchildren and their children when the polar caps melted and the coastal areas flooded? Would the waters reach into North Alabama, Tennessee, and Kansas? Would my grandchildren have enough food to eat when the ground became so poisoned that crops wouldn't be fit to eat and half the species of plants and animals became extinct? What if the tainted water made them sick? What would be left except concrete, steel, and plastic?

Okay, Gayle, writing isn't happening. Get a grip. Eat something. Do something. But what? The house was a mess, the dog needed walking, dinner had to be cooked, but I couldn't bring myself to move.

Retirement wasn't working for me; I should've had my novel finished by now, and Heather should be well on her way to solving her problems. My pen scratched a few lines across the paper. It drew arrows going in both directions, wrote a few words like, "Heather needs a place to live," but nothing else came to mind. Then, for no reason at all, I began to draw pictures of Woody Woodpecker, something my brother had taught me to do when I was in second grade.

Sometimes, and that day was one of them, my mind crawled back into that little girl and again looked up to her big brother, hearing him admonish her to "think." I watched him as a teenager push a boy in a wheelchair through a museum, often picking him up so he could see the mummies or ancient masks of pre-Columbian Americans. Again, he and I sat at the dining room table while I cried and told him my childish tales of another misfortune while he listened, patiently, as if that was the only problem in the world at that minute in time. As an adult, he worked with teens at-risk for becoming delinquents. He said the pay was low, but his job satisfaction was high.

Brother was only eight years old when he was diagnosed with childhood diabetes, and he passed away at forty-two from complications of the disease, but he'd done more in those years to help other people than most of us do in a lifetime. He was more than my brother; he was my confidante and friend. If only I could see his face or hear his voice or whistle as he went about his daily life. If only.

No longer able to sit still, I wandered into the guest bedroom and turned on the television. My fingers tapped their way through dozens of TV channels with boring images in glorious living color and annoying people saying dumb things. I flipped through books and magazines; the words stared at me in a meaningless jumble of black letters on white paper; the ads with pictures of perfectly shaped, air-brushed beauties mocked me. What I needed was a walk, but those huge dark clouds threatened imminent rain. Wind rattled the branches of the leafless crape myrtles, and it was only forty degrees.

I strolled to the kitchen, opened the refrigerator, and stared at its contents. It was filled with sinful leftovers. The turkey and dressing most likely were past their prime, but the chocolate pie, now that was probably still edible. I shouldn't eat it, though. Too fattening. Not healthy.

I ate it. Then guilt settled in. Starving children in Africa. My arteries probably clogging that very minute. I could have a heart attack, and Clay'd have to miss part of a game to call the paramedics who wouldn't get there in time because they, too, were watching football.

Sure, I could diet and try to lose the holiday weight I'd gained. I might even write a few words, but who was I kidding? Nothing had been good enough to publish. In the fall I'd sent out two short stories to dozens of publications but had heard nothing. And Heather was nowhere near the end of her journey.

Of course, I *did* finish my memoir, and years ago I'd had a couple of nostalgic pieces published. Surely that meant something. Both were about my original family. The first piece, published in *The Birmingham News*, was about my mother's last Christmas.

I knew the holiday season of 1989 would be her last, but I couldn't bring myself to admit it, and none of us could talk about it. She knew it, too, but her thoughts weren't on herself; she was worried about my stepfather, Chick, whom my children affectionately called Pawpaw.

"He's having a hard time right now," she'd said. "I wish we could do something special for him."

And we did. On Christmas Eve, my children and I pulled out his old Army uniform along with dozens of photo albums. We listened to Mother's stories, the ones he'd told her about his mother, father, siblings, and childhood and his time in Germany during World War II. On Christmas Eve, we had him sit in the chair of honor and performed our *This is Your Life* special.

Each child was someone from his past. Scott appeared as young Pawpaw wearing his old Army jacket with "42nd Rainbow Division" and a rainbow stitched across the sleeve. We told his stories, showed him the pictures of his life, and reintroduced the love of his life as Mother made her grand entrance. It's still the most memorable Christmas of my life. And when I think about it, I still cry. The next October, after a valiant struggle with cancer, Mother passed away. Her last Christmas had been the end of an era for me.

I was jolted back to the present when Clay yelled something from the den about a fumble. I remembered Brother in his Bear Bryant hat and how much he and Mother had loved football. I went into the den and sat beside my husband. As we watched the last half of a game between two teams I knew nothing about, I wiped at tears that wouldn't stop seeping into my eyes.

Later that New Year's Eve, while Clay watched a different game, I baked a frozen pizza and took a couple of slices to him. I was blessed to have him and my children and grandchildren. I made up my mind to get out of this down mood if it killed me, and I'd start with a few New Year's Resolutions. Back to the dining room and notebook.

First goal: Spend more time writing and finish my novel. Second Goal: Lose weight, exercise more, and eat less. Wait. Weren't those the same goals I'd written the year before? And the year before that? Yes, but in my heart I knew this year would be different. This year I had time on my side.

I might've thought of some more goals, but Clay walked in at that point and, while pouring orange juice into his glass, launched a new bombshell into my life. As nonchalantly as if he were commenting on the weather, he said, "I think I might retire this year." As I tried to process this pronouncement, he turned and walked back to his television.

I sat there, bewildered, scared, unable to move. I'd barely begun to enjoy my freedom. I pictured him standing over me while I vacuumed or dusted, telling me what to do but not offering to help. I'd be at the computer deep in thought, words for my novel pouring into my head, and he'd come in and say, "When's lunch going to be ready?" I'd never be alone again! No, he couldn't retire.

thirteen

THE JOY OF TOGETHERNESS

He retired. On his first full day of freedom, in the middle of a long stretch of gloomy, cold, cloudy late-February days, what did Clay do? Celebrate by taking me to lunch? Shopping in the morning when the stores weren't as crowded? Visiting friends? No, he wanted to clean the garage. I didn't help. Instead I used that time to write.

Heather had finally left her husband, and he was absolutely livid. He accused her of having another man all along. He'd show her and the other guy. I stopped and stared at the computer screen. Hadn't I read this abusive-husband, wife-tries-to-get-away story hundreds of times before? Seen it on TV and in movies—the same story in different forms and characters? What made Heather's story different?

Worth telling? How could it help other women in the same situation?

From the garage I heard thumping, bumping, and bangs, followed by a few choice words. I ignored all of it, but I couldn't concentrate. And my stomach growled.

A chicken sandwich and some chips might help. Quietly, though I didn't think he could've heard me above all the noise he was making, I slipped into the kitchen and opened the refrigerator door. A crash from the garage. I waited to hear a moan or a scream, but hearing nothing, I continued to make my sandwich and sat at the counter to eat.

I swear the man has radar. Before I got the first chip in my mouth, he barged through the door and asked, "What're you eating?"

"A sandwich."

"And potato chips and onion dip," he said. "I thought you were on a diet."

"And I thought you wanted to live."

Totally oblivious to my mean mood and thoughts of mayhem and destruction, he made himself a sandwich, sat beside me and dipped his potato chips in my dip. "I need help in the garage."

I stared at him. I didn't want to clean the garage. Heather was at a crucial point and needed me. I wanted him to go to work so I could be alone and think. Besides, his idea of cleaning the garage was to move all the stuff back into the house that I'd moved out of the house into the garage.

"I'm going to put all the Christmas stuff in the attic," he said.

"Why? You'll just have to get it down next December."

Now he was getting agitated. "You going to help or not?"

Reluctantly, I agreed. It was the start of a routine. He started projects, asked me to stop whatever I was doing and help, and I did. Poor Heather was left dangling so many times that she and I despaired of her ever getting her happy ending.

Two weeks later the garage was cleaner than the house, and one morning Clay woke up, went to the YMCA to work out, and never again mentioned the garage. Nor did he clean it again.

He did, however, try to help me. When I was sweeping, he pointed out the spots I'd missed. When he walked past the cat's bowl, he said, "The cat's bowl is empty."

"When I see it empty," I replied as nicely as I could, "I pour more food in it."

"Well, she needs it now," he said and walked away.

Leaving our poor, faithful Pumpkin without food, I shook my head, walked into the bathroom, turned on the shower full force and screamed.

Clay and I are from the era when women burned their bras, marched, and demanded their rights. I wish

I'd marched. I don't live with my children, so I don't really know, and maybe they don't do it on a daily basis, but I've noticed my sons and sons-in-law cooking, cleaning, and helping with the children. Charles always cooks breakfast for me when I visit them. And when I've taken my grandchildren to the pediatrician's office, there are always more grandparents and fathers there than mothers.

Back when I took my own kids to the doctor, the only man in the whole office was the doctor. Now even the doctor is a woman. I love these younger people and this time to be alive. My mother and her friends were supposed to stay home, like Beaver's mother, and clean house in high heels and pearls.

When my friends and I went to work, we were supposed to be supermoms, those powerful women who could work, do all the household chores, take care of the children, cook delicious dinners, and fall into bed, amorous and beautiful. I think we were also the first generation of women who fled marriage in droves and tackled single motherhood.

Oh well. I figured I'd probably never make Clay over into my image of him, so one morning a few weeks into his retirement, I decided to quit nagging. During breakfast, while he read the paper and totally ignored me, I grabbed my notebook, sat down at the dining room table, and wrote three words. The newspaper shuffled and rattled, and Clay said, "The real estate market in Birmingham isn't improving," and before I could say anything, stuck his head back into the paper.

I stared at my last sentence, trying to remember that great string of words, that literary genius I'd been ready to add to the sagging middle of my ongoing saga. The genius had vanished. A word came to mind. A scene. I could almost grasp it.

"I can't believe it," Clay said. "That townhouse on Hampstead sold for practically nothing. It was in good shape, too. We should've bought it."

I didn't answer. I couldn't answer. Without a word, I grabbed my notebook and stomped to the guestroom/office to transfer what I'd written into the computer. He never noticed my frustration and later that morning asked if I'd like to go out for lunch. Of course, I always wanted to go out for lunch. Anything to not have to cook.

The thing was he didn't have a clue. He knew making the bed and occasionally moving clothes from the washer to the dryer was his sole duty as far as housework was concerned, and he did it. Without complaint. He never complained about anything, not even my cooking or forgetting, never raised his voice or put me down in any way. He was courteous, kind, even-tempered, and responsible. If he didn't know how to help with the house, well, that was such a minor thing, not worth a minute of my attention. We were going to have a great retirement together.

By spring I got used to having him around, and we settled into a routine of sorts. He slept late so I could have my early morning coffee, back porch conversations with birds and foliage, and writing time. Of course, I still sometimes used that time to relive the past and worry, and sometimes I actually worried about worrying so much.

If I kept that up endlessly, what would happen to me? Would my brain turn to mush? Would I start to drive to the dentist and wind up in Chicago? Would I do it during football season when no one would miss me until after the Super Bowl? If I quit worrying about my children, would they be able to get through their days without mishaps and live their lives productively and happily? What would happen to the world if I didn't worry about climate change and how everyone needed more love and manners and politeness in their lives?

In my heart, I was pretty sure that everything and everyone would be fine. But just to be certain, I set aside a few minutes each morning to write my prayers for my family, friends, and the world around me.

fourteen

PAGES AND POUNDS

As the one-year anniversary of my retirement approached, I realized I'd actually accomplished a few things. Not weight loss, of course, but I had written a short story about my unsuccessful dieting attempts that banished fad diets from my thoughts, hopefully, forever. The story came to me one day when I was thinking about the Thanksgiving dinner Cathy had cooked years ago for her then-new in-laws and Clay and me. The table was perfectly set, dinner was prepared to perfection, and everyone used their company manners and made polite conversation. I don't think Charles's parents even noticed the situation with the pumpkin pie. At least, they've never mentioned it.

MASSACRE AT THE BASKIN-ROBBINS

I gave up dieting during the Clinton administration, the night my perfect cousin Connie called and invited herself to dinner. Unfortunately, my husband, Roger, answered the phone.

"Why didn't you ask me?" I wailed. "I'm tired and my feet hurt." As I jerked cans and boxes from the cabinet, the tomato paste fell and smacked my big toe. Usually I don't curse, but right then a string of words I didn't know lived inside my head spewed from my mouth.

"Just relax." He snatched the last piece of lemon pie from the refrigerator, sank into his favorite recliner, and said, "I'll keep her company."

Oh, yes. Big help. He'd talk while I cooked and cleaned. "You'd think her house was falling down the way she calls you every other night to fix something: her washing machine, disposal, air conditioner. I liked it better when we only saw her for Christmas and Thanksgiving."

He ignored me and touched the remote. President Clinton looked me straight in the eye and vowed he hadn't slept with that woman. Quickly, Roger changed channels and became absorbed in the weather report. That should've been a clue.

I clenched my teeth and clutched the handle of the skillet. In an instant I had it perched to pour its scalding contents over his head when who should slither in the back door? Skinny Princess Connie. Completely oblivious to me and my intended mayhem, Roger jumped up and almost hit the skillet with his head. Spaghetti sauce splattered all over me, the stove, and floor. Nothing landed on Roger, of course.

"You look great," he said to her.

Looking up from the floor I was cleaning, I smiled and promised myself I'd lose weight even if it killed me.

It almost did.

I tried everything, from the drinking man's diet— even though I don't drink—to the grapefruit diet. Nothing worked, and the constant gurgling and churning in my stomach might have made me a tad cranky.

"You've got to stop all this nonsense," Roger said one day as I cried into my dry salad. "Eat like a normal person and you'll lose weight."

I wanted to seize his baked potato stuffed with cheese, bacon bits, and sour cream and smash it into his face.

"It's all those diet books. Stay away from them, you hear?"

"You don't understand."

"No, you don't understand. Just eat like a normal person."

"Easy for you to say. You could eat a whole cow and a box of chocolates and still be thin."

He ignored me.

The next time I went to the bookstore, I headed straight for fiction. I passed the new arrivals and classics, but the closer I got to health and self-help, the slower I walked.

From two aisles away, the book jackets and magazine covers beckoned me. This is the last diet you'll ever need. Lose the weight and keep it off—forever. Eat all you want while the pounds and inches melt away. As I reached for one of the forbidden books, a hand tapped me on the shoulder and a syrupy voice cooed, "Jolene?"

Like the time Mother caught me licking the "Happy" off Great-Gramma's 90th birthday cake, I jumped, and as I swung around, my hand, accidentally of course, hit Connie on the side of the head.

"Sorry. You okay?"

She nodded then gave me one of those hugs sorority sisters do even if it's only been ten minutes since the last time they saw each other and said, "Want to go to the food court and grab a bite to eat?"

Sure, like I wanted to be zapped with a bolt of lightning. "Love to," I said, wishing just once she'd have a bad hair day or her lipstick would smudge so that when she smiled, her pearly white teeth would have a bright red streak on them.

"Going on a diet?"

"Huh?"

"You were looking at diet books."

Caught. And she'd probably tell Roger. "I was thinking about it." Surely there was at least one pimple she'd tried to hide with makeup or dark roots or a clump of gray in her blonde hair.

"Just eat a little less," Connie advised between bites of her super-deluxe, extra cheese pizza. "That's what I do."

"But you're not fat."

"I'm disgusted with myself." Her left hand patted her stomach as she looked around to see if anyone was within hearing range. She leaned so close I could smell her pepperoni breath when she whispered, "I weigh 115 pounds."

"Wow, that much. How awful for you." Should I kill her now, I wondered, or run over her in the parking lot? I'd wait for the parking lot, but I might as well finish my burger and fries first.

"I think I'll stick with my low-fat diet." She stuffed half a slice of pizza into her mouth.

Yes, maybe that would work for me too. After all, dieticians, heart specialists, and all health magazines spouted the benefits of low-fat. So I bought a book that listed fat grams in food and rushed off to the grocery store. Love those food manufacturers. I found low-fat cakes, cookies, ice cream, puddings, and sour cream. Spent $148.79 that day. But it was worth it.

"Mom," my daughter, Natalie, said one day as I ate an entire fat-free apple-spice cake and washed it down with Diet Coke. "I don't think you're supposed to eat the whole thing."

"Sure I can," I answered between bites.

"But it's got 100 calories a slice." She snatched it out of my hands. "And you've eaten ten slices."

I grabbed it and hit her with the wrapper.

For breakfast the next day, I had two bowls of shredded wheat with skim milk. Good for me, very little fat in that. For lunch I had a plate of vermicelli, smothered in fat-free sour cream and low calorie margarine, two biscuits I had made with low-fat baking stuff, and a low-fat blueberry pie. Sometime around two o'clock, I began to feel hungry and so tired that I hung my head over the computer and slept—until Roger came home from work and shrieked, "You been dieting again?"

"No."

"Then how come you ate the whole pie?" He picked up the empty aluminum pan and shook it at me.

"Leave me alone."

"If you'd listen, I could help."

I glared at him, the meanest stare I could muster, and dared him to say it.

He said it anyway. "Just eat like a normal person."

I gained twelve pounds on that diet. So, I decided to try one of those low-carb, high-protein diets. Lost seven pounds the first week. Finally, the perfect diet.

One night in the middle of the third week, Roger, Natalie, her husband Josh, and I sat down to dinner. Without looking my way, chomping and chewing, laughing and talking, they devoured their pinto beans, mashed potatoes, and cornbread. I stared at my lonely pork chop. Did they care about me? Not one bit.

About that time my sinister pork chop smiled a mischievous, sarcastic kind of smile, and a slice of cornbread sat up on the corner of its plate and winked. I swear it did, and then it laughed. I'll show you—you cornbread you. With my knife, I stabbed it over and over until it was crumbs. Then I threw the pork chop across the room and pinto beans at the wall.

There's a blank disc in my brain between that minute and when I suddenly realized I was sitting at the table alone—eating the last bites of the red velvet cake. I found Roger, Natalie, and Josh in the family room surrounded by white bags with golden arches. When they saw me, they grabbed their Big Macs and fries and headed out the door.

The next night Roger seemed reluctant to sit down for dinner.

"It's okay," I said as he gingerly took his place at the table, looking at me the way one looks at a police officer who is standing beside your car window, pen and paper in hand. Smiling to reassure him, I added, "Go ahead. Help yourself."

"I can't take this anymore," he said. "I'm leaving."

"Fine, go ahead. See if I care."

"If you'd forget these stupid diets and eat like..."

"Don't you dare say it."

He didn't leave, and I promised to give up dieting and join a weight-loss class. Guess who was in charge of my group? Connie passed around a picture. "This is what I looked like when I weighed 125 pounds but look at me now. I lost ten pounds and have kept it off for more than three years."

I hated stepping on that scale. She studied the numbers, murmured, "Hmm," wrote something in a notebook, and loud enough for everyone to hear, announced, "165 pounds. Your goal is 135. Think you can do it?"

Three weeks later, ten pounds lost. The high of highs, better than a bag of malted milk balls. For this wonderful achievement, Connie smiled and presented me with a pink ribbon.

Then came Thanksgiving. Just a little pumpkin pie seemed so innocent. After all, I didn't even like pumpkin. Still don't know why I ate the whole thing. Natalie tried to stop me. As she smiled and chatted with her in-laws, who sat across the table from us, her hand inched its way toward the pie, grasped the edge and slowly, almost imperceptibly, slid it away from me. As I watched it go by, my fork, on its own volition and without any forethought on my part, stabbed her hand. Looking straight ahead, still smiling, she dropped the pie.

The next three weeks were a nightmare. One day I managed to stay on the diet, and the next day I ate everything in sight. Once, when I was trying really hard to be good, I ate Weight Watchers brownies. They were so luscious I ate two whole packages and if the wrappers had been edible, I'd have eaten them too.

Every time I weighed in, Connie shook her head, but smiled and said, "You'll do better next week."

And I did. Until the day I decided to reward myself with a small indulgence—an innocent vanilla ice cream cone from the Baskin-Robbins.

That's when I saw them. Like skinny teenagers, Roger and Connie smiled and gazed into each other's eyes as they shared a banana split with whipped cream and nuts. Her spoon clinked against his. His foot rubbed hers. She pushed a light brown curl from his forehead. My dinner almost came up.

I don't know exactly what happened after that, but I found myself leaning against the wall with my legs apart while a stout policewoman rubbed her hands all over me. The manager of the Baskin-Robbins was shouting something about a restraining order.

Connie lay on the floor with chocolate, vanilla and green mint ice cream smeared all over her body and matted into her shiny blonde hair. Strawberry ice cream was smeared across her pearly white teeth. Roger laid next to her with a chair across his head and his pants unzipped with—well, no need to go into that.

Strange thing happened after that. Connie quit calling or coming by. When I saw her at our family reunion, she ran the other way. And Roger never again mentioned the word diet, food, or eating normal.

After I paid for the damage to the ice cream store and promised not to get within fifty yards of it, I gave up dieting and haven't lost or gained weight since. Come to think of it, now might be a good time to try smaller portions and exercise more. I know I could do it. I think I'll start now. Right after I finish this last piece of pecan pie.

Although the story is fiction, my struggle with dieting and weight loss was real and frustrating and depressing. On the low-carb diet, I really did fantasize about eating things like cornbread, pinto beans, and grits, in addition to cake, ice cream, pie, cookies, French fries, fast food, and sweet potatoes. It was in the middle of that phase of dieting that I succumbed and had a slice of pumpkin pie at our Thanksgiving dinner. And another. And another. That's when my own daughter tried to, without being noticed, slip the plate from my hands. Now, ordinarily, I would never intentionally hurt one of my children, but I was under supreme diet duress and forgot who and where I was. I saw my pie try to get away, and my fork really did stab her in the hand. She dropped the plate and I got the last piece of pie. If her in-laws, who are now friends, noticed, they've never mentioned it.

I wish I could say that after I wrote the story I was able to eat normally, lose down to a size six, and live in skinny bliss happily ever after. When I can do that, I'll write another book. However, I did accept that there is no magic pill or diet that will make you lose weight, but why should we all be skinny anyway? I'm healthy, my cholesterol, blood sugar, etc. is normal, and my husband, children, and grandchildren love me and my twenty-five extra pounds. My other great discovery? I feel better when I eat less, especially sugar, and go to water aerobics, the second most fun way to get exercise.

fifteen

HEALING

Thankfully, my writing was going better than my dieting. I'd completed a memoir and given it to my children for Christmas, written a few short stories and poems, and I was working diligently on my novel. Though I knew it would need lots of editing and revisions, the process of writing a 300-page novel had been tiring, stressful, liberating, and exhilarating. I'd laughed, cried, and wallowed in nostalgia and anguish. Finally, the writing had exorcised many of the residual demons of past failed relationships and helped me forgive not only the people who'd done me wrong but also myself for doing them wrong.

I've even forgiven my father for not being there for me when I was a child and understood that he'd loved me as much as he could in the only way he knew how.

As I reread what I'd written, I realized that Heather, my heroine, was struggling with some of the same things that had plagued me. Of course she did. She was me. But she was stronger, able to understand the situation, and confront it.

At my current age, I can see how little girl Gayle felt and how she could have handled things better. Then, however, all she knew was that her dad had left and rarely came to see her, and that she missed him and his friend playing the guitar and singing "You are my Sunshine" in the front yard. She missed his fake-surprised, funny face when she and her mom picked him up after work and she popped up out of the back seat. She wondered what she'd done wrong. Was she not pretty enough?

While still a preschooler, the older boy down the street took Heather into the woods and molested her, and she had to go into a courtroom and answer the judge's questions. Although I have absolutely no memory of this, my grandmother and mother told me about the same thing happening to me. I do remember that the boy avoided me and ran whenever he saw my brother. I also remember biting him so hard that he bled, and I ran home, afraid I'd be in trouble.

Heather played hide-and-seek with the neighborhood kids and paper dolls with her best friend. Little girl Gayle did these things also, but more often she stayed in her room, alone, anxious about something; she didn't know what. Her favorite thing was a Mother Goose book that she carried with her, like Linus carries his blanket.

Heather was afraid to be away from her mother for any long stretches of time. What if she left too? Unlike little girl Gayle, she was able to go to her cousin's house and spend the night without worrying about whether or not her mom would be there when she got home.

I was never raped, but when I was thirteen, I did have an encounter with an older man, a trusted friend of the family, who tried to. He had his hands all over me. I fought and ran, but I never told anyone. At the time, I was worried it would have hurt my family. Heather was raped, but, unlike me, she told her mother and later in the novel she tied the guy to a tree and set it on fire. I could never actually do something like that, but writing that scene gave me great satisfaction. And guilt for thinking it.

When I finished writing the novel, I knew it was not a story that was publishable or that I would ever want anyone else to read. It was me, venting all those emotions, fears, and failures through Heather. What she learned, I learned. Who she was able to forgive, I forgave—and gained insight into my relationships with men. I longed for a soul mate, someone I could talk to about anything, whose values were like mine, and with whom I could share fun, laughter, and love. But surrounding me was an invisible, impenetrable wall of anxiety that no man could get past. It dawned on me that I was partly to blame for every failed relationship, and, though it took a while, I was able to let go of some of the anger and resentment I felt toward all men. Except, of course, my brother, stepfather, and two sons, and sometimes even they were on my hit list. There are times when the old fears and anxieties seep into my memory and I relive the scenes and the old bitterness resurfaces, but I don't stay there all the time. I understand that I can bless the person and let go.

Heather was beginning to understand all of this too, and she was ready to put the past behind her and move on.

"What're you going to do in your new life?" I asked her one day as we sat in lawn chairs in the back yard, letting the sun's rays shine on my arms and legs and produce Vitamin D in my body.

Her body was always pretty much translucent and barely there. I had to keep reminding myself that she was purely a fabrication of my imagination.

"You tell me," she said.

"Law school, maybe?"

She thought for a minute and shook her head. "No, I don't think so."

"I know. Children. You want to work with children."

She smiled. "Yes, that's it. That's what I've been trying to tell you. And I want to go home."

"Home?"

"When this book's finished, I want to go back to my cabin by the Little Pigeon River."

"That's right. You've never told me how you really felt about your life in the 1800s."

When I first encountered Heather, I was a single mom—tired, depressed, not knowing which way to go, how to keep the bills paid, how to get through the nights, or how to find the energy to get out of bed. One early morning, sometime between midnight and dawn during one of my sleepless nights, somewhere between sleep and awake, I dreamed that I sat on a rock beside the Little Pigeon River, my feet dangling in the flowing water. The forest surrounding me was thick, lush, and green. The sky was sunrise peach and gold. Frogs and crickets chirped, birds sang, the water was cold to my toes, but the air was warm and humid. A salamander crawled up on the rock and then quickly scuttled away. I picked up a few flat, blue pebbles and tossed them into the stream.

On the other side was a log cabin in a clearing. A young woman wearing a long, gray dress opened the door and walked outside. Her eyes were red as if she'd been crying, and her light brown hair was pulled into a bun at the back of her neck. Tendrils clung to her face and forehead. She carried a child, who appeared to be two or three years old. Its head, arms, and legs hung limply toward the ground. She reached across the river and handed the baby to me.

I jerked awake and lay there, trying to figure out what that vision meant. I'm still not sure. After that she appeared to me frequently. Sometimes I went with her to the cemetery and watched her put flowers on a tiny grave with a pile of rocks for a headstone, one of them engraved with the words, "My Angel."

My visions of her, though, weren't always sad. One time she gave me tips on make-up and hairstyles. Other times, she was inside her one-room cabin with her husband, a tall, dark-haired man wearing a red plaid shirt, who sat at the wooden table reading the newspaper while she cooked over an open fireplace. Small children played and laughed and chased each other, sometimes stopping to cry and hit and shout. His eyes and attention never wavered from his reading. Her face was moist with sweat, and her damp hair stuck to her temples and forehead. Hmm. Some things never change. There definitely was a story there.

"Ok," I said, "Next novel, I'll take you home."

sixteen

THE REDBIRD'S MESSAGE

In mid-July, the day before the anniversary of my retirement from the working life, I sat on the back porch to watch the sunrise. It was spectacular, with delicate spun-gold clouds against a peach and gold sky streaked with tinges of orchid pink. The azaleas had long ago lost their white and red flowers, but my roses were in full bloom, and their fragrance mixed with the scent of cut grass and filled the air. I searched for my redbird but found sparrows and robins instead. I closed my eyes and tried to clear my mind, listen to the sounds of nature, and meditate, but my spring optimism had vanished, and I couldn't get my thoughts to slow down.

For the better part of a year I'd spent my days running errands. And when I did find time to write, I spent it sitting on the back porch, waiting for the muse to strike and trying to recapture the youth of my children. I talked to redbirds and ghosts. And they talked back. I was a mess. What in the world was wrong with me? No wonder Mother had thought she had to take care of me my entire life. No wonder she had clung to me as if I were a part of her that might escape and do something wrong if she loosened her grip.

As I gazed at the crimson roses, I sensed her floating toward me, her Chanel No. 5 arriving before she did. She set her ethereal cup of coffee on the picnic table and smiled.

"What I wouldn't give for a whiff and a taste of that," she said.

I sipped my French vanilla concoction, smiled, and said, "I miss you so much."

"What would we talk about if I were really here?" she asked.

"I'd tell you my life is finally the way I dreamed it could be."

"Then why are you so down?"

"I don't know."

"Because something's missing, isn't it?" She paused. I couldn't think of an answer, so she added, "But you can't quite put your finger on it?"

"How did you know?"

"Mothers know."

"At least you did. You always seemed to know what I should do. I never did," I said.

"You know you have to let your children go and quit living in the past. They're all well-adjusted, mature adults."

"Like you let me go?" I asked cynically.

"Is that what you want for your children?"

I shook my head. Deep inside I knew she was right. "But I don't know how."

"Neither did I."

At that moment I understood. For most of my life I'd felt like she and I were in a struggle for control of my life. So much contention. All because neither of us could let go. As the early rays of sunlight fell softly across my arm and the side of my face, I magically became a child again and Mother was young and beautiful with long, chestnut hair, sparkling blue eyes, a quick smile, and hearty laugh.

She, Brother, and I again ate dinner in the tiny kitchen of our two-bedroom apartment in a low-rent area. As she washed dishes, I dried and Brother put them away. I heard her say, "I see something you don't see. It's red and starts with a c."

I looked around. Something that started with a "c."

"Cup?"

"We don't have any red cups."

"The cut on Gayle's arm?" said Brother.

Mother grasped my arm and examined the microscopic wound. "How'd you do that?"

I shrugged my shoulders.

Brother called out impatiently, "Curtains."

"Those curtains are beige."

"But look at that red thing right there."

Mother looked at the smudged streak, then at me. "Have you been trying to add color to the apartment again?"

While inspecting the floor and my scuffed saddle oxfords, I shook my head.

She laughed and pointed to a corner on the floor where I'd dropped the sleeveless nub of a red crayon, "Then how did that get there?"

Busted.

She handed me a white soup bowl that had contained canned tomato soup a few minutes earlier and started singing, "*Bill Grogan's goat was feeling fine.*" We joined in, "*ate three red shirts right off the line.*"

Those days must've been hard for her—being a single mother when that was a rare and much frowned-upon thing. She supported us by working as a cashier at the old Hill's Grocery Store, but we didn't know we were poor. She often gave Brother and me a dime each to spend on whatever we wanted. Sometimes I bought an ice cream cone, but most of the time I bought a "funny book," usually Archie, Jughead, Donald Duck, or Bugs Bunny. I had a stack of them almost to the top of my closet.

"It wasn't as hard as you think," Mother said to me as the memory faded.

"But you worked so hard for so little pay," I said. "And you had nothing to show for it."

"I had you and Brother."

I longed to hold her hand and tell her how much I appreciated and missed her, that despite all the turmoil and upheaval of my childhood, she'd made it fun and I always knew she loved me more than her own life.

"Remember how Brother always woke up whistling and smiling?" I said.

"Yes," she said, "and you woke up like an angry zombie."

"His early-morning cheerfulness made me mad."

"As I recall, your kids were a lot like you."

And, as always, my mind went back to when my children were young, to the time we lived in that small town close to Chicago.

Again, I shouted to each one of them, "I told you ten minutes ago to get up! You'll miss your bus!" And again, they rolled over and groaned.

We sat on the floor around the Game of Life while Ginger and Smokey, our dogs, jumped on the board, scattering the pieces. My children built an igloo in the backyard—a snowman in the front. They lay on the frozen ground and carved angels' wings into the snow. As I had done so many times, I too lay in the yard watching the snow fall on me, my arms and legs slowly waving across the ground, the cold flakes gently falling into my eyes, on my eyelashes and lips, and melting on my face and in my hair. It was the most beautiful, peaceful place on earth.

Diana and Darrin shoveled snow, and when they came in I made hot chocolate for them. For an hour I dressed Cathy and Scott in their long underwear, snowsuits, scarves, socks, boots, and gloves. They went outside, threw a few snowballs, rolled a few into tiny snowmen, and ten minutes later ran into the house yelling, "I'm cold!" I made them hot chocolate too.

I remembered tiny hands giving me flowers picked from the neighboring yards for Mother's Day. I remembered lacey cards made at home and school with "I Love You Mommy" scribbled on them.

As if reading my thoughts—well, Mother probably did know my thoughts—she said, "You've got to get busy, do things you enjoy today. Live today. It's okay to occasionally look back, but you can't stay there. And you can't depend on your children to give your life meaning."

I stared at the empty chair, the place I'd imaged my mother sitting, and heard her words, but I knew they were my words, in my head, and it was what I'd wanted from her. I had to, I could, and I would give that to my children. Let them go. Hold them in my heart? Yes. Constantly relive the past? No. Constantly worry about their safety and welfare? I'd try not to. And I'd try, really try, not to make them feel guilty if they couldn't make it home for Christmas. I closed my eyes and tried to visualize my life without worry and anxiety.

When Clay came out, the sun was shining brightly, and the clouds had dissipated, but Mother had vanished. The overwhelming heaviness I recognized as depression enveloped me and tears seeped out of my eyes. I needed her. But she was gone forever. I'd never again feel her hand on my forehead and hear her voice pronounce me "feverish" or "cool."

He hugged me and asked, "What's wrong?"

I smiled through tears and said, "Nothing."

"I know something's wrong." He sat in his reclining lawn chair, maneuvered the plastic wrap from the Sunday Birmingham News, and turned to the sports section.

I couldn't answer. He'd forgotten the question. For at least an hour or so neither of us said anything. He read. I loitered in my past, longing for something, I didn't know what. Maybe some connection to my original family. Something to fill the empty place inside me now that I'd no longer be worrying about my children or reliving their childhood. Something to give my life meaning.

Later that morning, after much persuasion, Clay agreed to go with me to Nectar in Blount County, where Mother grew up and where many of her relatives are buried.

To get there, Clay drove north on Highway 79 through the small, recently-incorporated city of Pinson, where my father and his brothers and sisters grew up. When I was young, Pinson had been a tiny, rural area, and Highway 79 was a long, winding two-lane road that meandered through pastures, fields, and farms. I wondered what it'd been like when Daddy was growing up there in the 1930s on a hill they called "Sasfras Ridge." Was it like Walton's Mountain? Were my dad, aunts, and uncles like the Walton children?

Daddy's mother, Mama Lap, as everyone affectionately called her, had been a widow with five children to raise. She said they often didn't have enough to eat but "the Lord always provided." I'd listened over and over to the stories of her children growing up, the funny ones, with them misbehaving and acting up, and begged for her to tell them again.

During the Depression, though she barely had enough for her own family, Mama Lap not only shared food with the local African-Americans, she invited them in and let them sit at her table. An unthinkable thing in the South in the 1930s. One that could have gotten her hurt or worse. She always said "underneath our skin we're all the same."

I closed my eyes and pulled up an image of Mama Lap and realized I looked a lot like her. She was short, a little overweight, and had the same gray hair I'd have if I didn't color it. I wish I'd asked her about her parents and what it was like when she was young. All I knew about her early life was that when she was a baby, her mother and father had died the same day, hours apart, of influenza. She'd been raised by an aunt, I think. If only she'd shared her own stories and wisdom in a written record.

I was grateful I'd written my stories down and given them to my children and grandchildren. Maybe some of them would appreciate it; maybe they wouldn't. But I was glad I did it. Hopefully, they would be able to see that their ancestors were not just abstract people, but real, honest, hard-working individuals, who lived, loved, made mistakes, laughed, and cried.

At the old country cemetery in Nectar, every grave clean and decorated with fresh and plastic, mostly red and white, flowers, I pointed out to Clay my maternal grandparents, cousins, aunts, and uncles who'd gone before me, and told him about my mother's father.

He'd died of colon cancer when I was nine. In his last few months, even though he was tired and sick, he, as always, let me climb on him and comb and curl his hair. He laughed and played with me. One of my earliest memories is of him in the garden he'd planted in our backyard on Greenwood Street. Brother and his friend had picked okra, and Granddaddy hosed them down to get rid of the chiggers.

Later, as the sun was setting, and trees darkened against a sky streaked with brilliant pink and purple, Clay drove silently south on Highway 79 toward home. Beautiful words and nostalgic thoughts filled my mind, and I was sure I saw Heather and Mother in the back seat. I smelled Mother's perfume and heard them laugh and talk.

"She made it through the first year," Mother said.

"Yes, she's going to be alright now," Heather answered.

They were right. I'd be better than alright. After all, I'd already written a memoir, and Heather had almost completed her journey. I'd finish her story and send it off. I knew I could do it and Mother confirmed it. "You can do anything you set your mind to," she said.

The next morning, on the first anniversary of my retirement, I grabbed my first cup of coffee and went straight to my computer. I meant to hit the Word icon, but before I knew it my fingers had punched Facebook, and then I figured I might as well check my emails. For some reason I hit one of my favorites: book publishers. Well, since I was there I might as well search to see who published novels. No, I should go to the library and bookstore and get a few books to read that were similar to mine.

I started toward the bedroom to get dressed but noticed I'd left some cinnamon rolls on the kitchen counter. I stopped abruptly. The voice in my head that urges me to do unhealthy things said, "Yummm. Take a bite." The other voice that sounded a lot like Diana said, "Don't do it. You know you'll regret it later." I gazed at the cinnamon rolls, inhaled their nostalgic aroma, and in a few minutes was back in Mother's kitchen with my young children and Pawpaw.

Mother closed the oven door and before she could get the gooey rolls from the cookie sheet to the waiting brown stoneware plate, five pairs of hands started grabbing them. I resisted.

"Go ahead," Mother said. "One won't make you fat."

"Okay," Without further hesitation, I stuffed a bite of the warm sweetness into my mouth.

Scott laid his cinnamon roll back on the plate, ran into the den, and started pushing his yellow Tonka truck around the room while making those growling car noises that boys are born knowing how to do. Darrin and Cathy grabbed for the same one.

"That's mine." Darrin jerked at the roll, which pulled apart and left him with a tiny piece.

"Okay," Cathy said as she took most of it with her and ran to the back porch to join Scott.

Diana ate hers slowly. "I wonder how many calories are in this thing," she said. "And probably my whole day's worth of fat and salt."

Mother and Pawpaw glanced at each other and smiled as they ate theirs. They'd grown up during the depression and often didn't have enough to eat. They never forgot to appreciate every meal.

As Mother's kitchen receded and mine came back into focus, Diana's often-repeated words stayed with me, "Do you really need that? You need to eat more veggies and exercise more."

I wrapped the cinnamon rolls in plastic wrap and hid them in the back of the refrigerator. After I scrambled an egg and ate it, I took my notebook and cup of coffee and retreated to the back porch. I'd done it. I'd faced one temptation and, with the help of my daughter, won. My next hurdle: meditate without worrying about my children or living in the past.

Yes, I'd certainly come a long way in a year, sitting on the back porch, sipping coffee, not worrying about Diana and Cathy driving from different directions toward Birmingham, not wondering if they'd had their oil checked and tires rotated and balanced before they left, hoping they hadn't forgotten their cell phones. Yes, not worrying gave me time to think about my next book and Heather's new adventures. Even though for the second time, a car had left the highway and crashed through the front of the building where Darrin worked and barely missed hitting him, I wouldn't worry about whether or not the county would fix that road or if Darrin could at least move his desk. I was sure he'd be fine. And I wouldn't fret about Scott and his family driving all the way to Disney World that night, even though he'd forgotten to send me one update on their progress or texted me that they'd gotten there. No, it was great not to worry.

As my mind drifted from Scott to Heather, I gazed at the birds crowded on and under the bird feeder: the finches, robins, and sparrows, side by side, sharing their abundant supply of seed. If only humans could do that. That's when my friend the redbird landed on the feeder and pecked at a couple of sparrows. They flew away. Oh well, so much for sharing.

As if reading my thoughts, the redbird looked toward me and didn't move. I stared. He stared. Maybe, he was trying to tell me something—an important message of some sort. I closed my eyes and listened. Immediately I heard a voice, as clear and loud as if she was right there beside me, scream, "Help!" On the inside of my eyelids, as if in a motion picture, Heather clung to a raft as it bobbed up and down and raced downstream toward a waterfall. I could feel the dank air, see the dark, ominous clouds and hear the roaring thunder while lightning lit up the sky. On the bank of the rushing river, Mother jumped up and down, her arms flailing, yelling, "You've got to save her, Gayle! Hurry!"

Quickly, I grabbed my pen and notebook and started writing.

THE IMPOSTER

I do not recognize her,
So young and free.
Laughing, crying, pretending to be me.
She tries to run away.

Plays hopscotch on the sidewalk,
Wades through gutters, and
Drives a car across the bridge
Without looking back

The tears and laughter and black sunshine.
She plays house with dolls that cry
And dishes that break.
She clutches her soul and watches it float away

Before she waves goodbye
And starts up the hill,
Whispering words I do not hear
And cannot understand.

I try to follow and catch a glimpse
Of this child who stayed a while
And disappeared into the fog
On the other side.

Sometimes, I think I see her, waving
And laughing, beckoning, and daring me to find her.
Almost I feel her warm breath
And touch the air that surrounds her.

ABOUT THE AUTHOR

After being a legal assistant for many years, Gayle Young retired to pursue the calling she had found when her sixth-grade teacher picked her play to be performed by the class: writing. She has published short pieces in newspapers, anthologies, and magazines. *Redbirds, Roses, and Ghosts* is her first book-length work, a humorous, heartfelt memoir about the challenges of becoming a writer. Her most important role is wife to her husband Larry and Mom and Nana to her children, grandchildren, and dogs, some of whom appear, reluctantly, in her writings.